Moonstone And Mistrust

by

Marie Higgins & Stacey Haynes

Copyright © 2023 Marie Higgins & Stacey Haynes

All rights reserved.

ISBN - **9798398992106**

people had stared at her as she passed them, not only aghast that she would dress this way, but because she wanted to catch up with the filthy drunk. She didn't care what others thought of her. Thankfully, she had moved away from that stage in her life.

Narrowing her eyes on him, she tightened her legs around the horse's belly, pushing the animal faster. Within seconds, she would be close enough to capture the man. She couldn't figure out why he would want to run from her unless... Perhaps he was Hawk's accomplice in the bank robberies between southern Utah and Longmont, Colorado, where she felt the man was hiding. And her hunches were usually spot on.

When she was nearly close enough to touch her horse to Jeremiah Jones' animal, she pulled out her rope. Since she had been taught to rope cattle from the time she was in pigtails and old enough to climb on a horse, she was always prepared for the chance to do some calf-tying, even in this case she considered it *bandit-ropin'*.

Alexa let the rope fly through the air until it wrapped around her target. With a hard tug, she tightened it around the man as she brought her horse to a stop. The quick movement yanked the unsuspecting drunk off the animal, dropping him to the ground with a hard thud.

She jumped off her horse and rushed toward him. Naturally, he would be struggling to breathe since the wind had been knocked from his lungs, but that gave her the seconds she needed to roll him face down in the dirt, and finish tying his arms and legs behind him.

Grinning, she nodded at her work. Indeed, she was good at capturing outlaws.

"What...are ya...doin'?" the man questioned in between large gulps of air.

"You left before I was finished questioning you." She chuckled to herself, loving her answer. Sometimes she found her wit was used more than her ropin' skills.

"I told ya. I don't know anythin' about Hawk."

"And I told you," she rested her boot in the middle of his back, holding him down on the dusty ground, "I know

"I'm sorry to make you remember that part of your life, but I can tell by your reaction, that you *do* know my brother. Please, help me find him."

Growling, he yanked his arm away, and her hand dropped to her side. Malice turned his brown eyes darker. "Leave me alone. I told ya I don't know him, so quit buggin' me."

He moved past her, drunkenly weaving his way toward his horse. She wasn't about to let him get away.

"Mr. Jones. You're the only one who can help me."

"Then yu'll never find yer brother."

Although she didn't tolerate people's snarky attitudes, she would put up with his for a few more minutes as she tried to wear down his resistance.

"Please, Mr. Jones. You cannot possibly leave without giving me some clue as to where my brother is staying. That is all I need. Just some direction."

It was a good thing she had been searching for the man named Hawk for six months. After all, looking for bank robbers was something she did best… Well, at least one of the things. Yet, she needed to get Jeremiah to talk. The trail had led her to this town and to Jeremiah, so she mustn't let him get away.

Alexa reached him before he mounted his horse. She grabbed his arm, keeping him from going anywhere. "Please don't make me beg."

He glared and pushed her away so hard she fell backward and landed on her rump. The pain wasn't as bad as the humiliation filling her. How dare he accost her in such a way! This man didn't deserve her sympathy, and now it was time to show him what kind of woman she really was.

Jeremiah Jones climbed on top of his horse and took off as though the devil rode on his heels. Thankfully, she had a fine horse that had been trained to race. One of the main reasons she purchased Pegasus was because the animal was fast.

Alexa quickly mounted and rode after Jeremiah, following him even as they left the town. It didn't matter how many batting her eyelashes and pretending to be a helpless female would have to be part of her plan.

"Excuse me, can you help me?" she began politely. She might be dressed as a man, but she remembered how to be courteous.

"What do ya need help with?"

She still wished she could remove his cocky expression. However, that would come later. From her investigation, she discovered that Jeremiah Jones had lived in Utah six months ago and had worked in Big Ed's mines from the time he had been kidnapped as a child, to adulthood. Alexa also found out that he knew one of the lead men called Hawk. Apparently, that was the name everyone called him.

"I'm looking for my brother." She hoped God would forgive her for lying, but she needed to get Jeremiah Jones to talk. "You worked with him in the mines, and now that the whole country knows about Big Ed kidnapping children, I need to find my big brother."

Disgust molded his expression now. He lifted his chin and folded his arms. "If ya don't mind, I'd like to put that nightmare behind me."

"Please, Mr. Jones." Hesitantly, she placed her hand on his dirty shirt. "My brother is the only family I have."

Jeremiah blew out an exasperating breath. "Fine. Who is yer brother?"

"We called him Hawk." Alexa wished she had learned the man's true name, but Hawk was the name everyone at the mines used.

Jeremiah's eyes widened and his face lost a little color. "I've never heard of him."

It didn't take a genius to know the man was lying, but now she wanted to know why he was afraid of Hawk. Then again, in her research, she learned that Hawk had been one of Big Ed's lead men, which meant, the man supervised the other kidnapped children in the mines, and he probably even kidnapped some of them. Had Hawk tortured these poor lost children as well?

ONE

There was a reason she wore trousers under her dress. It kept her from sliding all over the place when she rode astride. Men's trousers held her legs against the horse better, and she would have words with anyone who disagreed.

Alexa Moore leaned closer to the horse, tightening her grip on the horse's reins as she narrowed her gaze on the target. The imbecile actually thought his horse was faster and that he could get away. He would know soon enough that although she was a woman, *meek and timid* were not words one used to describe her. In fact, once she caught the man, she would show him how unladylike she could be.

Being raised a tomboy certainly came in handy. Especially now.

Not more than fifteen minutes ago, she had stopped Mr. Jeremiah Jones as he stumbled out of the saloon. She nearly went inside the establishment to confront him, but there were a few things she wouldn't do, and being seen in a place like *that* was one of the no-no's on her list. So, she waited for Jones to exit the saloon before she moved in front of him, stopping him from proceeding down the boardwalk.

His glassy gaze roamed over her slowly, from her long, braided hair, down over her man's shirt and vest, and then continued to her trousers and boots. His eyebrow arched as confusion etched wrinkles on his face. Seconds later, his mouth stretched into a sly grin—one she wouldn't mind slapping off his face.

Perhaps she would teach him some manners on the proper way to treat a lady, but not now. She needed information, and otherwise. You worked in the Utah mines, which means you know Hawk who was one of Big Ed's lead men. There is no way you can tell me you have never met Hawk, when all the children and men who worked at the mines knew each other quite well."

She really wished she had more than just one name to give him. Was Hawk his first name or last? Or had it just been what the men called him at the mines? Eventually, she would find someone who could give her the right answers.

Jeremiah groaned, turning his face away from the dirt. "I don't know him personally. We were never friends."

"I find that hard to believe, especially when I was told he is here in Longmont, and surprisingly, so are you." She applied pressure to the foot on his back.

"But I don't know where he is."

"So, you're telling me that you just moseyed up to Colorado from Utah on a whim?"

"Well...not exactly."

"Then why are you here?"

He groaned. "To find employment, just like the rest who worked for years at the mines."

Alexa rolled her eyes. Usually, she was able to get drunken men to confess by now. Her skills must be rusty. She would certainly work on them.

"You have one last chance to tell me the truth. Where is Hawk?"

"What will ya do to me if I don't tell ya?"

"I'll turn you over to the sheriff."

"What for? I've done nothin' wrong."

"I beg to differ, Mr. Jones."

He struggled to move, but the pressure of her foot on his back kept him down. "What is my crime?"

"You..." She quickly thought of a good reason, even if it wasn't something men were jailed for—at least they weren't there for long. "You assaulted a lawman."

Jeremiah snorted. "I did not."

"Indeed, you did. You pushed a Pinkerton agent to the ground and ran away."

"Prove it," he snapped.

Sometimes, men were so obtuse. "The backside of my trousers is still caked with dirt."

He stretched his neck, turning his head more to look at her. "Yer not a Pinkerton agent."

"I sure am, and I have the badge to prove it." Using her foot, she added more weight on his back until he cried out. "Now tell me what I want to know."

"Fine." His chest heaved heavily. "I was told Hawk works for old man O'Leary at the Blue Creek Ranch. That is why I'm here. I want him to get me a job workin' at the ranch."

Alexa grinned wider. Once again, she got her man.

She loosened the rope enough to remove it from Jeremiah's body. He slowly rose to his hands and knees, cautiously watching her.

He arched a bushy eyebrow. "Yer just gonna let me go?"

"Yes, with a warning. You are to leave immediately. If I see you even come close to making contact with Hawk, I assure you, a jail cell would be preferable to what I'll have in store for you."

"Yes, ma'am." He scrambled toward his horse, mounted, and rode away, heading back into town.

She slapped her palms together, smiling. Perhaps she shouldn't have threatened him like that. After all, it wasn't as though she could actually follow through with her warning. By nature, she was not a mean person, but if one pushed her to the limits of her patience, they would see her wrath.

And she wasn't exactly a Pinkerton agent, either. Not yet.

Alexa wrapped up the rope, arranging it for when she needed to catch another outlaw, and hooked it to her saddle. She always wanted to be prepared. Life's cruel lessons had taught her that she never wanted to feel helpless again. Her three-month marriage to a man who didn't love her had only made her stronger and determined to be independent. But it was when her father's bank was robbed and the outlaw's horse ran over her brother, crippling him, when she decided to dedicate her life to bringing justice to bad men like Hawk—the very man who destroyed her family.

She mounted Pegasus and rode toward the direction Jeremiah had pointed. She had been in the area for a week now, had memorized where buildings were in town, and especially those ranches on the outskirts of town. She couldn't take chances with Hawk getting away. Out of all the outlaws she had captured in the last year, Hawk was more important. This particular criminal would not get away, if she could help it. Eating and sleeping came second to finding Hawk.

As she rode toward Blue Creek Ranch, her mind swirled with ideas of what she could do to catch the man. Obviously, he wasn't going to confess to robbing banks for the last several months, so there must be a way to find the proof without his confession. Of course, once she found the proof, he would have to tell her the truth.

Alexa felt sorry that he had been kidnapped as a child and forced to labor in the Utah mines for all those years. But once the corruption had been uncovered and the children were released, it was up to them to find good jobs and live better lives. True, some of the men only knew how to steal and cheat, but they were given a second chance in life, and Alexa expected Hawk should have considered his blessings and made the most of them.

Some outlaws never learned.

For her to find the proof she needed, Hawk must not know about her true intent. In that case, she should approach him as someone in need of help, but of course, she couldn't tell him the same story she had told Jeremiah. And no matter what, she couldn't show him her independence. Most men didn't approve of women who thought for themselves, anyway. So, as difficult as it would be for her to act that way, she must.

Perhaps she could play the part of a woman in distress who had lost her family during their long journey. After all, he wouldn't believe that she chose to be alone.

Ideas popped into her head of tales she would create about her make-believe life. She was certain they would grow into a bigger web of deceit the longer she waited to find evidence needed to arrest him. But it was something she had to do.

In the distance, a ranch came into view. Alexa quickly stopped her horse and dismounted. She dug through the satchel tied to her saddle for the one skirt she had. If she were to portray a well-mannered woman, she had better look the part. She quickly stepped into the skirt to hide her trousered legs. Adding to her appearance, she removed the band holding her braided hair, and ran her fingers through the waves, causing her long hair to flow over her shoulders and down her back.

The cool wind blew against her, reminding her that the sun would be setting very soon, and in this weather, she needed a coat. Unhooking the thick rolled-up garment from her saddle, she slipped her arms through the heavy material. Now she was ready to begin her disguise.

When she mounted the horse to ride astride, she rearranged the skirt to hide her pants. If, by chance, someone noticed, she would tell them she wore the man's garment to keep her legs warm. After all, this was Colorado, and it became cold at night.

Thankfully, she had arrived before dusk, so at least she could spy on the men working at the ranch to find her target. She had received different reports about his eye color. Men said his eyes were hazel, but women had mentioned his eyes were a dreamy green. She also heard that his shoulder-length hair was black, and that he was strong like an ox. Then again, descriptions could be distorted in six months' time. Maybe his hair wasn't long anymore, and maybe he wasn't as muscular as he had been while working at the mines.

As she rode closer, three men worked on the wooden fence bordering the property. Their shirts held sweat stains around the neck and underarms, and their trousers were snug quite nicely to their thighs. It was difficult not to notice how very vigorous they appeared. And handsome. In fact, one of the men stood out more than the other two. He was taller, and more robust, but it was his eyes that caught her attention when he looked her way. They sparkled like the sun hitting a mountain stream on a serene, summer's day. Although she couldn't be certain, she thought they might be green.

The man straightened and removed his hat. The other two men realized a woman was in their presence, so they copied the actions of the first man.

"Pardon me," she said sweetly, "but I hope you can help a woman in distress."

They nodded and said *certainly* at different times. She smiled, enjoying the way they appeared love-struck. Now she wondered how long it had been since they talked to a woman. There would have to be some women servants on a ranch as large as this one. After all, who would do the cleaning and cooking?

"I have lost my family," she began her fib. "I think they traveled this road, but I cannot be sure. They would have passed this way two, maybe three hours ago."

The man with the snapping gaze, stepped closer to her horse. His hair was jet black and longer than most men she had seen. Could this green-eyed man with the muscular body be the outlaw she was searching for?

"Miss, we have been working on this fence for most of the day, and I'm sorry, but there hasn't been anyone pass by. In fact, you are the first person to ride by the ranch."

Alexa frowned, and brought her hand to her throat, trying to appear distressed. She must play the part of a helpless woman in order for them to believe her. "Oh, dear. Then I don't know what to do."

A second man stepped toward her, holding his hat to his chest. "Miss, can you tell us how you got lost?"

"My family was traveling toward Colorado Springs, but Ma realized we needed more flour. I headed back toward the town we passed, while they continued going forward. I told them I would catch up." She blinked as though she struggled with tears. "But I think I got lost." She shook her head. "Actually, I *know* I'm lost."

The handsome man with the green eyes glanced toward the horizon. Night would be upon them soon, which would work in her favor.

He looked back at her. "Miss, I'm sure Mrs. O'Leary won't mind if you stay the night. You won't be safe by yourself out after dark. In the morning, we could help you find your family."

The other men nodded, wearing hopeful expressions. She tried not to grin in victory. So far, her plan was working well.

"That would be wonderful." She managed a shaky smile. Perhaps she should have made her career working as an actress in the traveling theater company. "My name is Alexa Moore."

"I'm Trevor Dalton," one man said.

The third man grinned. "I'm Zack Dalton." He pointed to Trevor. "We are brothers."

"Nice to meet you." She moved her gaze to the handsome man. "And you are?"

"You can call me Ash." He winked.

Her heartbeat flipped from his flirtatious gesture, but at the same time, her hopes dropped a notch. If he wasn't Hawk, could he tell her where the man was? Hopefully, Jeremiah hadn't lied to her about Hawk working at this ranch.

"Nice to meet you, Ash."

He motioned with his hand toward the ranch. "Come with me. I'll take you to the main house and introduce you to Mrs. O'Leary."

Ash moved away from her and closer to his friends before mumbling something to them. He stepped toward three horses that had been tied to a tree, and quickly mounted one. As she followed, her heartbeat quickened. First things first, she would find the bank robber, and then she would get to know Ash a little better. It had been a while since she spent time with a good-looking man.

Maybe her trip to the ranch wouldn't be wasted after all.

TWO

Ash Hawk stopped his horse in front of the main house and dismounted. As he moved toward Miss Moore to help her down, he couldn't stop from staring at her lovely face. She had the kindest eyes, and the sweetest smile. He hadn't seen a pretty woman since he met his friend's sister, Charlene six months ago. But Miss Moore was vastly different from Ben's sister. Although they were both slender, Miss Moore was taller than Charley. And Miss Moore's hair appeared to be a blondish-brown color. Of course, since the sun was descending, it was more difficult to tell her true hair color.

He reached up his hands. "Here, let me help you."

She smiled and leaned down, placing her hands on his shoulders. As she slid off the saddle, he grasped her waist. She didn't smell as flowery as Ben's sister, but Miss Moore had also been riding in the sun most of the day, trying to locate her family. He was certain Mrs. O'Leary would allow the stranger to clean up, and perhaps the older woman might have clothes that were made more for a woman. Although Miss Moore wore a skirt, her shirt and vest were definitely men's garments. And had he detected trousers under her skirt?

"You don't know how much I appreciate your help," she said as her feet touched the ground and she stepped back, breaking their contact. "You are too kind."

"What kind of gentleman would I be if I left you for the wolves and bears to feast upon?" He grinned. "Because we are so close to the mountains, most men wouldn't dare to travel by night, so I won't allow a woman to do so, either."

"Mr. Ash—"

"No, just Ash."

She nodded. "Ash, you are certainly a gentleman."

He took the reins from both horses and tied them to the post. He motioned with his hand for her to go up the porch's steps first. She did, and he followed, but moved ahead of her to open the door. She stepped inside and stopped. Her gaze roamed the hallway as her eyes grew wide.

Ash didn't want to laugh, but he had the same astonishment when he first entered the main house because it was vastly different from what the outside looked like. But Mrs. O'Leary kept her home sparkling clean, and richly furnished. He had only been in a few homes, but this one was the fanciest. Apparently, the ranch made more money than Mr. O'Leary led his workers to believe.

"What a lovely home," Miss Moore said softly.

"I thought the same thing when I first came to work here." He smiled. "If you'll wait here, I'll find Mrs. O'Leary."

He stepped past her, but she touched his arm, stopping him. When he met her wide-eyed gaze, his heart melted. The poor woman looked so lost and alone. He definitely understood that feeling, and he never wanted to experience that again.

"Do you think my family is looking for me…out in the dark?"

He gently took her hand. "Miss Moore, I'm sure they are worried, but if your father is wise, he would not travel at night."

Her smile trembled slightly. "My pa is very wise."

"I promise, first thing tomorrow morning, I'll help you search for them."

"You are a wonderful man, Ash."

Gratitude filled him, making him straighten his shoulders. He wasn't used to receiving heartfelt praise. Not in his miserable life.

"And you, Miss Moore, are too kind."

Slowly, she pulled her hand out of his grasp. Inwardly, he groaned. How could he have forgotten that he was still touching her so personally? Then again, he had never been taught polite manners when it came to a lady.

He motioned with his hand toward the parlor. "If you would like to sit and wait, I'll fetch Mrs. O'Leary."

"Yes, of course."

As she turned to enter the room, he hurried toward the kitchen. At this time in the evening, the boss's wife would be preparing supper for the crew. The woman was always on the go since she had only one person helping her with the meals and cleaning. All the men on the ranch lived in their own quarters and were responsible to wash their own clothes, but Mrs. O'Leary did everything else.

The scent of roast filled the air, making his stomach grumble. He would never get used to eating like a king, especially when he had been working in a mine since he had been kidnapped at the young age of ten. All of the children who grew up working in the mines ate scraps, while Big Ed and her lead men ate well. Of course, as he grew, he realized what it meant to be one of Big Ed's favorites, which is what he finally became.

Thankfully, Ben's sister showed up when she did and rescued them all. Charley would always have a special place in his heart for that very reason.

Ash found Mrs. O'Leary standing at the counter, mashing potatoes in a bowl. The woman was made for hard work since her arms were nearly as strong as most of the ranch workers. Although the tall woman kept an immaculate home, she was rarely seen with styled hair or wearing fancy gowns. She and her husband went into town on rare occasions, but when they did, they wore their finest clothes.

He stopped just inside the kitchen. Would the woman welcome a stranger into the house, especially a pretty one? Mrs. O'Leary wasn't what a man would consider *lovely*. She was tall and big boned. Her hair was short and curly, but her facial features were far from being feminine.

She swung toward him and hitched a breath. That woman had better hearing than anyone he knew.

"Forgive me for interrupting you," he said, "but you have a visitor."

She arched a bushy eyebrow. "I do?"

"Yes." He stepped into the kitchen a little further. "As the Dalton brothers and I were working on the fence, a woman stopped to ask for help."

Her eyes widened. "A *woman* is here...by herself?"

He nodded. "She was separated from her family, and she wondered if we had seen them pass by. Unfortunately, we couldn't help her."

"So, why is she here? If you didn't see her family, why would I see them?"

He chuckled. "I'm sorry that I'm not making myself clear." He swallowed hard. "But it's dark now and she is traveling by herself. I told her of your good graces and that you wouldn't mind if she stayed the night."

Holding his breath, Ash prayed he had sweet-talked Mrs. O'Leary enough to allow Miss Moore to stay.

The middle-aged woman wiped her hand on the apron tied around her thick waist. "Well, since it's dark, I suppose it wouldn't be Christian-like to turn her away."

He slowly released his breath, relived that Mrs. O'Leary didn't try to argue with him. "She is in the parlor."

Mrs. O'Leary scowled. "You don't expect me to keep her company, do you?"

"Of course not," he quickly replied. "In fact, if you need her help, I could bring her to the kitchen."

"Why would I need her help when I can do it myself?" She puffed out her chest, proudly.

He mentally kicked himself for saying that. The boss's wife certainly was the type of woman who always needed to be praised for her accomplishments. "Forgive me, I didn't mean it that way. I just thought you could put the stranger to work while she is here."

Within seconds, a light beamed in the older woman's eyes. "You know, that isn't a bad idea."

Once again, he breathed a sigh of relief. "Then I'll bring her back."

"Make sure she washes up first."

"I will," Ash said, hurrying out of the room.

He didn't know what it was about Mrs. O'Leary, but he found it difficult to talk to her. Perhaps he was overly complimentary, but then he wanted to make her happy. He loved working on the ranch, and he didn't want to give her or her husband any reason to fire him. He was certain his insecurities stemmed from those horrible years working for Big Ed. The woman made all the children at the mine feel worthless.

When he neared the parlor, he noticed Miss Moore slowly walking through the room, eyeing every statue and trinket Mrs. O'Leary had purchased over the years that held a special meaning. He watched Miss Moore closely. How could he not? She moved so elegantly, and used a gentle hand when she touched a few objects.

He could only study her profile, but she was certainly one beautiful woman even with the dirt smudges on her face and untidy hair. He still wondered why she wore men's clothes, except for the skirt, of course. Yet it didn't matter because she mesmerized him regardless.

Miss Moore stopped at one of Mrs. O'Leary's favorite paintings of the mountains in springtime. The Colorado mountains would look like that painting very soon, and the land would be scattered with blooming flowers.

Miss Moore tilted her head and leaned closer to the painting, as if searching for something. He guessed she was trying to find the painter's signature. Silently, he chuckled. He too, had wondered who painted such a beautiful resemblance of the mountains, but there was no signature.

"I hope you don't strain your eyes too much," he said, walking into the room.

She jumped and turned toward him. Her cheeks bloomed red as if he had caught her with her hand in the cookie jar.

"Oh, I didn't hear you, Ash."

He stopped next to her and pointed toward the painting. "I saw you looking at this and I wanted to let you know there is no signature. No matter how hard you try to find it." He switched his focus to her and smiled. "Because I have tried several times to find it."

She laughed. "Well then, I'll stop looking. It is a remarkable painting."

"Yes, it is."

She turned her head toward the painting again. "I don't know why, but it looks very familiar."

"Maybe it's because the Blue Creek Ranch is located in this area." He motioned with a finger on the lower lefthand side of the frame. "Whoever painted it must not have known about the ranch."

"Well, don't I feel silly." She folded her arms. "That must be the reason it looks familiar."

He turned toward her. "You have a cute laugh."

She hitched a breath and her cheeks bloomed with color again. "I...um, thank you, Ash."

Now he was the one embarrassed. Once again, he found himself tongue-tied and not knowing what to say while in a woman's presence. Then again, Miss Moore was difficult to converse with because she was so pretty. Mrs. O'Leary was just his boss's wife.

"I'm sorry if I embarrassed you." He shrugged. "Sometimes I say the wrong thing around women. I suppose it's because I'm surrounded by men on the ranch all the time."

"There are no other women here besides Mrs. O'Leary?"

He shook his head. "There is the cook, but there is no *young* woman at the ranch."

"Oh, I see."

A few awkward seconds passed in silence as her gaze moved slowly over his face and hair. He enjoyed her pleasurable expression, but it also made him realize how much he craved a woman's company. Of course, he wasn't the only one on the ranch. The other ranch workers probably felt the same way.

"Um, I found Mrs. O'Leary in the kitchen," he said.

"Oh, I'm sure she is really busy."

"She is, but she would like you to join her in making supper for us all."

Miss Moore's face brightened. "I would love to help."

"Splendid." He turned, and she moved beside him as they walked toward the hallway. "But I'll take you to get washed up first, if that's all right."

"Of course, it is." Her smile widened as she held up her hands. "I wouldn't want to touch food with these dirty things."

Laughing, he held out his hands. "Mine are dirtier, so I'll wash up with you."

Mrs. O'Leary had a special place on the back porch for the men to wash up before coming in for supper. As Ash opened the door for Miss Moore, the cool air slapped his face. The wind had picked up. He hoped that didn't mean a storm was coming. Then again, because of the season, he was sure they would be getting a storm soon.

As Miss Moore stepped out on the porch, she shivered and rubbed her arms. "I'm very grateful I found this ranch when I did. I wouldn't have been able to handle this cold wind without any shelter."

He stepped to the pump and poured water into the bucket. "I'm glad you found us, too."

She placed her hands into the water and quickly withdrew them. "That's cold."

"I'm sorry."

She shrugged. "It's not your fault." She took the bar of soap and scrubbed it over her skin before emerging her hands back into the water.

He found it interesting how much he liked watching her expressions change, and the different ways she smiled. In a way, he hoped they didn't find her family right away tomorrow. He wouldn't mind spending more time with her.

He handed her a towel to dry her hands, and then he proceeded to wash up. She gave him the towel, and he thanked her. Although shadows danced on the porch, he noticed she watched him a lot. He didn't mind at all, as long as she was comfortable with him studying her.

"Where are you from, Miss Moore?" he asked, stepping to the door and opening it.

"My family came from Utah. We are traveling to Colorado Springs because of my father's new job."

"Oh, really? What does he do?" Once they were inside, he closed the door.

"He is a banker."

He arched an eyebrow. "Really? Aren't there banks in Utah?"

She laughed. "Of course, but he will be managing the one in Colorado Springs. It's a promotion for him."

"Well, no wonder your family is in a hurry to get there."

"Yes." She frowned. "I just hope I didn't complicate things. I shouldn't have gone back to town by myself."

"Don't worry. There are only a few good roads to travel on, so I'm sure we'll find them."

"I pray you're right."

He led her down the hallway and into the kitchen. Mrs. O'Leary had cleaned herself up since he last saw her. Apparently, she didn't want to appear disheveled in front of their guest.

"Mrs. O'Leary, this is Alexa Moore, the woman who lost her family."

The middle-aged woman's gaze raked up and down Miss Moore's frame, and eventually, the woman's smile wasn't as genuine as it had been a moment ago. Confusion filled him and he wondered why Mrs. O'Leary wouldn't welcome another woman in the household.

"Ash has told me wonderful things about you," Miss Moore said. "And I'm very grateful that you are letting me stay the night. I assure you, I'll be out of your way first thing tomorrow."

Mrs. O'Leary's shoulders relaxed, and she nodded. "Well, the nights are cold, and I'm sure your small frame would freeze to death out there, so it's a good thing Ash brought you inside."

Miss Moore's attention moved to him, and she smiled.

"Ash has certainly been helpful, and I'll never know how to repay his kindness."

Her compliment made his heart skip a beat. Perhaps having her around was a good thing. Then again, she needed to be back with her family.

"Well…" Mrs. O'Leary's voice boomed in the room. "Miss Moore, if you're ready to *repay the kindness* I believe you can set the table for me."

Their lovely guest snapped her focus back on Mrs. O'Leary. "Of course."

"And Ash," Mrs. O'Leary continued, "you can ring the bell outside and let the others know supper is ready."

"I will." He gave Miss Moore a nod and moved out of the kitchen, happy that he was already washed up and ready for the meal so that he wouldn't have to fight the other men when it came to who would sit next to their pretty guest. He'd make sure he was right by her side.

It had been a while since the fluttering of excitement filled him, and he would take advantage of the little time he had with Miss Moore.

THREE

Alexa hadn't ever been in a situation where she was the only unmarried woman in a large group of men, and most of them were handsome and muscular. She was glad Mrs. O'Leary was in attendance during the meal, and that Ash sat next to her, acting like her protector.

Chuckling, she rolled out of bed and stretched. She had slept rather well for being in a different place, but at least the mattress was better than sleeping on the hard ground.

Mrs. O'Leary had given her a nightdress, and although it was four sizes too big, she was grateful that she didn't have to sleep in her clothes. Again. At least the woman allowed her to bathe last night, using flowery-scented soap. Since she had been a tracker, Alexa wasn't used to smelling like a lady. Perhaps after she caught Hawk and joined the Pinkerton Agency, then she could act more like a woman.

She threaded her fingers through her tangled hair, grimacing. There were many things she had skipped since deciding to become a Pinkerton. Maybe it was time to rethink her life. But first things first—Hawk must be caught and thrown in jail. Although it wouldn't heal her brother's legs, and it wouldn't repair the damage done to her father's reputation as a bank owner when the town stopped going to his place of business to deposit their money, but her goal was to make things right by arresting a criminal so he couldn't destroy any more lives.

Glancing toward the window, she frowned. What time was it anyhow? Usually, she awoke just as the sun was rising on the horizon. Yet from what she could see through the curtains, the sun hadn't made its debut.

She stepped to the curtains and parted them. The sky was still dark, even though there was a hint of light. That could only mean…

Sighing, she let the curtains fall back against the window. A storm was brewing. However, this could be a good thing. She still needed to find Hawk.

During supper last night, she wasn't able to meet every man who worked on the ranch. Mrs. O'Leary mentioned that some men went back to their bunks without eating, and of course, not all the men she met told her their name. Besides Ash, there were three others who had black hair and green eyes. Two of those men had shoulder-length hair, but she knew that in six months' time, the length of hair could change on a man, so she wasn't worried about that.

Alexa went to her saddlebags and found clean clothes and a brush. She would have to wear the same skirt since that was the only one she had, but everything else she was able to change. She brushed her hair while pacing the floor, thinking of ways to talk to the other three men who resembled Hawk's description.

Maybe if she feigned some type of illness, Mrs. O'Leary would be fine with Alexa staying another day. After all, if one is sick, they should not go out into a storm. And from what she gathered from Ash's personality last night, he was the type of man who would make sure a sick person stayed indoors to heal.

She chuckled. He was quite an interesting man. It surprised her that most of the men looked up to him, almost as if he was their boss because they acted as if he was the one to make the decision whether the other men could talk to her or not. Either that or they noticed that Ash had claimed her as someone he wanted to guard. She wouldn't mind that for a little bit, but she was sure that eventually, it would become tiresome.

Even though she didn't want to admit it, and no matter how charming Ash was, the fact remained, he had black hair and green eyes. That put him on her suspect list. Since she couldn't mingle much with the other three, she would start with Ash. After all, getting to know him on a more personal level might prove beneficial. There would be a possibility if Ash was not Hawk, he knew who it was.

Once her hair was brushed thoroughly, she walked to the window and peeked outside again. There was a little light in the sky, and just as she surmised, there were storm clouds, thickening by the second. Off in the distance, she noticed the mountain that was in the painting.

That painting! She couldn't be certain, but she knew she had recognized that scene from somewhere. If only she could remember. Yet it reminded her of Pa for some reason.

Shaking her head, she sighed. Hopefully, she could figure out why she felt this way, and why she was so interested in that painting.

After making the bed and stuffing things back into her saddlebags, she laced up her boots, grabbed her duster, and left the guest room. The house was quiet, except for pots clanking together in the direction of the kitchen.

She stepped quietly toward the room, and the first scent of food made her stomach grumble. Her hunger would have to be put on hold for now since there were more important things to do. However, she must make sure Mrs. O'Leary was kept busy before Alexa snooped through the house.

She stopped just outside the kitchen door and listened for voices coming from inside the room. Although she didn't hear voices, the clanking of pots continued to ring through the air.

Cautiously, she peeked inside. Mrs. O'Leary stood by the stove. Three large pots had steam rising from the top. Her stomach grumbled again, and she placed her hand on her belly. *Not now!*

As she took a step back to leave, something on one of the shelves on the wall caught her attention. The colorful, porcelain carousel with painted ponies, baby carriages, and sleighs, all on a wooden platform, made her think of when she was younger and with her family. Pa had taken them to a Founder's Day celebration that had one of the very first carousels in Utah. She had been intrigued and in awe of the very large toy that even adults enjoyed as well.

Since that day, she had seen many miniature porcelain replicas of the carousel, and seeing one in the O'Leary house made her homesick for some reason.

She tore her focus away from the carousel and moved away from the kitchen and from one hallway to the next until she was in the main hall. As she had waited in the parlor for Ash last night before supper, she studied the area for anything that looked out of place. Thankfully, that was one less room she had to snoop through.

The door was slightly ajar in the next room, opposite the parlor. Alexa glanced up and down the hall, making sure no one was watching her, and she slipped into the darkened space. Books lined the shelves on the wall, as well as small figurines of animals and people.

If Hawk was hiding among the workers, he would need a place to store the money and items taken from the bank's vaults. If she were the bank robber, she would hide things in plain sight, amongst other valuable items. From the looks of this room, there were many valuable items for her to study in hopes that she'd recognize them as being things that were stolen.

She placed her belongings on a chair before moving behind the desk to the books. She pulled a few out, checking to see if any bags of money had been stashed behind them or inside. It was a long shot, but as a future Pinkerton agent, she needed to cover all tracks. *And how did you catch them?* They would ask her. *By thinking like a criminal, of course.* Grinning, she put the books back in their places.

Of course, Hawk wouldn't put all his eggs in one basket. He would most likely have his own storage space where he could gaze upon the stolen riches. But he would place them throughout the house—a little here and there—just to make people not notice. Thankfully, she had a good eye to notice when someone was hiding something. That was why she could catch her thieves quickly.

Below the bookshelves inside the cabinet were two sets of drawers. Carefully, she pulled one open. A thick book that had bent pages captured her attention. The makeshift book held pages upon pages of what looked to be an accounting of outgoing money with dates written to the side of the amounts. At the top of the page was written in bold letters a man's name. *Employment records perhaps?*

She turned each page, which apparently was in alphabetical order. Anderson… Butler… Dalton, both of them… Farnsworth… Granger… Hall… Alexa's heart thumped faster as her fingers touched the next file… Hawk.

"What are you doing in here?" A loud voice boomed behind her.

Startled, she snatched her hand away from the book and jumped to her feet, facing the middle-aged man who had entered the room. Slowly, in hopes of not being noticed, she pushed the drawer back with her foot.

A large burly man wearing overalls, scowled at her. His black hair was short, which accented his chubby cheeks. She didn't recognize him from dinner last night. He was older than the other workers, but that didn't mean he wasn't one of them.

She gulped. "I—I was lost and saw this room. The books on this shelf intrigued me. I love to read and…" Alexa tried to think of more things to say.

"Who are you?" he snapped.

"Miss Moore," she replied. "And who are you?"

"You aren't to be asking the questions, I am." He stepped forward and she moved slowly around the desk, keeping her distance from him. His steely eyes frightened her, and his thick arms looked as though he could easily toss a tree.

"I'm very sorry. I will leave," she said.

"What were you looking for? I don't think you were in here looking for books." His eyes narrowed. If he were a bull, steam would be blowing from his nostrils, but she tried not to let that intimidate her. After all, she had taken down bulls before.

"I was curious. I haven't seen so many books in such a long time. Then those figurines caught my attention." She pointed to the porcelain figures. She continued backing away from the desk as he rounded to where she stood moments ago.

His focus lowered to the drawer she had opened. It didn't close all the way. She bit her bottom lip trying to think of what more to say to talk herself out of this mess. With his large boot, he pushed the drawer completely closed then his gaze shot up to hers.

"Who invited you here?" he asked.

"I did, Mr. O'Leary." Ash's calm voice broke the tension in the room. "She came by the ranch late last evening, in search of her family. I promised I would help her this morning." His gaze met her and he smiled. "I'm glad I found you, Miss Moore."

She wanted to sigh with relief, but she feared Mr. O'Leary would still demand answers. "Good morning, Ash."

Ash moved next to her, putting the much-needed shield between her and Mr. O'Leary. "I've been looking for you. I thought we were meeting in the sitting room before beginning our journey this morning."

This was the perfect cover-up for being in the hosts' study. "This isn't the sitting room? Oh, dear." She hesitated, more for emphasis. "Please forgive me." She turned her pleading gaze on Mr. O'Leary. "I honestly didn't know."

The man arched an eyebrow, and she couldn't tell if he believed her or not. But, if he was used to being around flighty women, then he wouldn't blame her. At least she hoped.

Ash chuckled and touched her shoulder. "Don't worry yourself, Miss Moore. This house is very large, and it's easy to get lost." He glanced at his boss. "Right, Mr. O'Leary?"

The middle-aged man harrumphed, flipped his hand in the air, and walked around his desk.

"We should go now," Ash said in a hurried voice as he gathered Alexa's saddlebag and duster. "The horses are ready."

"I apologize for not recognizing you, Mr. O'Leary. You really have a lovely home." She grinned, stepping behind Ash.

Ash moved her carefully out of the study. Now, she could feel relieved. Then again, would she have to convince Ash that she was absent-minded, as well? She hated the feeling of being unprepared.

From his appearance, she could tell he was ready for the weather conditions. He wore his black, felt Stetson, and a long black coat that was left unfastened. His clothes were clean and wrinkle-free, which told her that he either did the ironing himself, or he sweet-talked Mrs. O'Leary into doing it for him. Alexa believed the latter.

"Thank you, Ash," Alexa said, touching his arm. "I thought he was going to toss me out through the window."

"I'm glad I arrived when I did." His smile widened. "Or Mr. O'Leary *might* have thrown you out."

As they walked toward the door, his steps slowed. This time when he looked at her, his gaze was wary. "But I must know why you were in Mr. O'Leary's study. We really hadn't talked about where to meet this morning before starting our journey."

Inwardly, she groaned. Ash was too smart for his own good. "No, we hadn't talked about it, which makes me that much more relieved for your interference. I don't want the O'Learys to think I go around snooping through people's homes." She laughed lightly. "I was waiting for you, and was distracted with the lovely decorations."

His expression relaxed and he nodded. "They have some very fine paintings. I, too, found it addicting to stare at when I first arrived at the ranch."

"Then you understand me well."

"I do."

He reached the door, but before opening it, he helped her shrug into her duster. She buttoned up the front and pulled up the collar to keep her neck warm.

"Are you ready?" he asked.

She nodded. "I'm eager to find my family."

He opened the door and let her step outside first before following. She noticed he kept glancing up at the stormy sky, and by the time they reached two horses that had already been saddled, Ash was frowning.

"What's wrong?" she wondered.

"I fear we're going to get caught in the storm."

"Oh, dear." She sighed heavily, but more for show since she wasn't ready to leave yet. "Do you think we'll get rained on?"

He nodded. "But hopefully, it won't be terrible."

"Yes, I hope not, too."

He assisted her onto her horse, and within seconds, he had mounted his. He led the way, which relieved her. After all, she was still playing the part of the helpless female. But for the next few hours, she needed to ask him questions about Hawk, without appearing like she was trying to find the thief.

Hopefully, she could pull it off.

FOUR

The cool wind blew against Ash's face, stinging his skin. He lowered his head to keep it from freezing his nose, but he doubted it would help. The longer they were out in this weather, the colder it would get. Dark blue-gray clouds had blocked the sun rather quickly. He noticed that Miss Moore leaned over her horse to block the wind as well. They shouldn't have left the house. Thankfully, they hadn't been traveling long, so they could easily return to the ranch.

Every so often, he looked toward the sky. This was his first winter in Colorado, and he wasn't quite sure what to expect. Thankfully, those he worked with pointed out the different shapes of clouds and what each kind meant. The blue-gray clouds screamed snow, which he hoped wouldn't happen yet—not until he found shelter.

The incline of the road they were traveling on proved his snow theory. The temperature turned cooler, and snowflakes swirled in the wind. They had reached a point where he figured they wouldn't make it back to the ranch before they were engulfed in the storm. So, it appeared that he needed to find shelter soon.

Ash looked again at Miss Moore. If he weren't mistaken, he could see her bottom lip quivering from the cold.

"We need to get out of this weather," Ash called to her. "Do you trust me?"

Her gaze flew to his. "Of course, Ash. I know you won't let us freeze out here."

"Just over the ridge is a small cabin. If I remember correctly, it's abandoned, and even if it's not, I hope whoever is staying there will let us wait out the storm inside. Follow me." He shook the reins and brought his horse into a faster gallop, and Miss Moore kept up with him.

The snow became thicker as they rode more into the low-hanging clouds. He squinted his eyes, searching to find the correct path. He'd been this way many times in the fall looking for lumber with the other men. It wasn't that hard to find.

The howling of the wind through the trees made his ride faster. He could still hear Alexa's horse behind him, so he knew she didn't get lost. Up ahead the outline of the cabin came into view. He pointed in that direction.

"Go there," he yelled over the wind.

It seemed they were both anxious to get out of the weather, because within minutes, they were at the cabin. He climbed off the horse, and quickly helped her down from the other animal. Fighting against the bitter wind, he wrapped the reins around a small post. Ash would take them to the small barn once he and Alexa were inside the cabin.

Ash knocked on the door, but because there was no smoke coming from the chimney, he knew it was empty. He pushed hard on the door, and it creaked open. Alexa hurried inside, rubbing her hands over her arms.

"I'm going to put the horses away. I'll be right back."

"I'll see if I can start a fire," she said, looking around.

Ash quickly went to the animals and ushered them through the blizzard that was fully upon them now. Thankfully, there was enough shelter in the barn to keep the horses from the storm. He hurried and removed their saddles, throwing the blankets over the horses. Before heading back to the cabin, he grabbed both his and Alexa's saddlebags.

Alexa knelt in front of the fireplace tossing dry kindling in the pit. He put down their things, grabbed a few logs, and brought them over to her. It was nice seeing a woman who knew how to take control instead of waiting for the man to start the fire.

"I'm so sorry." Ash moved beside her on the floor and helped her place the logs in a tee-pee manner over the kindling. "I should have never taken you out of the O'Leary's home."

"Please, don't worry about it, Ash. I wasn't feeling very welcome at their home anyway. Mr. O'Leary frightens me." She scooted back. "I'm sorry for taking you away from the ranch because of my problems."

"No need to apologize. If we are stuck in the storm, your family is as well."

She frowned. "I only wanted to leave this morning so they wouldn't worry about me."

"I'm sure they are worried sick." He stood and ran his hands over the mantel until it stopped on what he was looking for and took the box of matches with dust covering the top. Hopefully they would still strike. "I'm sure they have found shelter and are praying for your safe return."

He kneeled back to the side of her and struck the first match. It lit up immediately. He put the burning match against the kindling to get the fire burning.

"I'm just very thankful that you are here with me. I would have died out here in the cold if it weren't for you."

He liked the way she praised him, even though he hadn't done anything yet. As the log burned, heat generated from the firepit. Ash stood, reached out his hand to assist Alexa to her feet. She slipped her cold hand into his, and he pulled her up.

"You are freezing." Out of instinct, he rubbed her soft hand, adding warmth to it.

"How long do you think we will be here?"

"Honestly, I don't know." He let go of her. "Mrs. O'Leary made some biscuits for our journey, so we do have some food if we get hungry."

Alexa wandered to the worn couch. She took her hand and brushed the cushions, stirring up a little dust. Alexa hesitated to sit.

"I'm sorry this place isn't cleaner for you." Ash spied a wool blanket on the shelf. He quickly grabbed it and shook it out. "Here, let's put this on the couch."

Moonstone and Mistrust

"Oh, I've been in dirtier places," she replied. "Have you?"

He let out a small huff and nodded his head. "For many years, in fact."

Alexa took the corner of the blanket and helped cover the couch, then she sat. She patted the spot next to her.

"We have lots of time." She smiled. "You might as well sit and tell me everything."

"Everything? About what?" He joined her on the couch. The springs groaned under their combined weight.

"Are you from Colorado?" She rubbed her hands together.

"No. I, too, have lived in Utah for a while. I was ten years old, I think, when I was taken to Utah. Just recently, I decided to make a move to find out what I'm good at doing." He didn't want to tell her all about the mines. That really was a time in his life he wanted to forget.

"Is building fences what you do best?" Her eyes sparkled as she spoke.

"I'm really good with my hands in building things. I'm a hard worker."

"If you could do anything else, what would it be?" She leaned her head back against the couch. His gaze dropped to her slim neck. Ash hadn't had that much experience with women, however that didn't stop the urges to want to snuggle against her and kiss her throat.

"I don't have much education, so just working on the farms is good enough for me." He shrugged.

"Don't sell yourself short." She rubbed her hands quickly. "You could own your own farm."

"I would need more money to do that." He reached over, taking her hands in his. He brought them up to his mouth and breathed warm air on them. The heat from the fire wasn't working fast enough, so he needed to help her from freezing.

"D—do the O'Leary's um, pay well?" she stuttered over her words as her cheeks turned a little pink.

"I guess. I really don't know what the going rate is for labor help." He rubbed her hands again. "Do you think we should move the couch closer to the fireplace?"

"If we do, a spark might set the couch on fire." She laughed lightly. "That wouldn't be very safe."

"Not at all," he replied. "But your hands are so cold." He brought them to his mouth again and breathed on them.

"Maybe, we should sit closer to each other. Our body heat could warm us." She didn't wait for him to reply, but instead slid closer.

He swallowed, adding moisture to his dry throat. Her leg touched him and sent a comfortable vibration throughout his body. His heart thumped rapidly. Ash wasn't sure if she was flirting with him or not. The men at the farm would take him into town to talk with the single ladies there. Never once did a woman's touch excite him as Alexa's was doing right now.

"If you think so," Ash replied. He turned his attention to the window to take it off the beautiful woman sitting next to him. The snow swirled all around and the flakes were huge. "I don't think it's going to let up anytime soon."

"I hope you won't be in trouble for not returning to the O'Leary's ranch. I didn't mean to take you away from them." Her hand wiggled against his. If he weren't mistaken, it felt as if her fingers were caressing his palms.

"There are others on the ranch. I shouldn't be missed today."

The fire crackled, sending a spark flying out onto the floor. Ash jumped off the couch and stomped it out. It would be terrible if the cabin caught on fire right now. He grabbed another log and tossed it on the fire.

"This cabin sure is drafty," Alexa said. "Whose place is this anyway?"

"It belongs to Mr. O'Leary, at least that's what I had been told. From the looks of it, he hasn't been here in a long time." He brushed his hands on his trousers. "Come here by the fire. You need to get warm."

Alexa stood, rubbing her arms, and walked over to him. Out of instinct, he put his arm around her to keep her warm. Her body stiffened slightly, then her shoulders relaxed, and she stepped closer.

"I think the quickest way for us to get warm is to use our body heat," she whispered. "Are you opposed to that?"

He gulped down a hard swallow and shook his head. "No, Miss Moore. We need to stay warm any way we can."

"Ash," she said, sliding her arm around his waist. "You can call me Alexa. I'm fine with that."

He turned, pulling her into a bear hug. Alexa's body fit perfectly with his. Her hair smelled like fresh lilacs, the fragrance of the body soap that was in the O'Leary's home. That was one of his favorite smells. Her hands slid inside his open coat, warming her fingers.

Already Ash's body heat was rising, but not enough to want to let her go. He was enjoying her in his arms. She snuggled against his chest, and his breathing grew ragged.

"Are you getting warm?" he whispered.

"Getting there." Her sultry voice sent exciting tingles along his neckline.

Ash knew what would warm them quicker, but he doubted she'd want to kiss him. They barely knew each other. Yet kissing her was the only thing on his mind. No other words would do. Besides, if they found her parents, he would never have this chance again.

He rested his face against the top of her head. The flowery scent surrounding her drifted by his face. He closed his eyes, relishing the moment. Ash moved his hands across her back in soft circular movements, and her hands copied the motions against his back.

"Alexa, do you have a beau?" he asked. Ash needed to make sure he wasn't kissing some man's woman. He didn't need a cowboy to come looking for him.

She tilted her head and looked up at him. Her smile was beautiful. She slid her right hand up the front of his chest until it rested on his shoulder.

"Not anymore." Her fingers moved to his hair, and she gently twisted a lock in between her fingers. "Do you have a girl?"

His heart thumped harder. Ash couldn't keep his gaze off her pink lips. An invisible magnet pulled him toward her as he moved his face closer. She stayed still. Perhaps she wanted his kiss after all?

"The only girl I have is the one I'm holding right now." His lips brushed her forehead with a small kiss. "I'm just wondering if she would let me warm her more."

Alexa's lips parted slightly as she pushed on the back of his neck, bringing him down. As soon as their mouths met, he gently kissed her. He wasn't an expert at wooing the ladies since he'd only kissed two girls in the last six months. Hopefully, his inexperience wouldn't be a disappointment.

"Warm me," she whispered on his lips.

A jolt of passion pushed him eagerly into another kiss. He followed her movements as their lips danced together.

FIVE

Why am I doing this?

Alexa must stop this before it became too late. After all, he was her suspect… wasn't he?

She threaded her fingers through Ash's hair, enjoying the soft little moans coming from him. She hadn't been kissed in such a long time and now being in his arms, she didn't want to pull away. Not yet.

Occasionally their teeth would bump awkwardly against each other, but that didn't stop the passion of the kiss. Ash must be the thief because he was stealing her heart at this very moment.

Ash was the one to break the kiss so he could gaze into her eyes, giving them a quick minute to catch their breath. He had the deepest green eyes she'd ever seen. She didn't want their passionate moment to end, and she prayed he could read her mind.

A small smile pulled at the sides of his mouth, as if he knew exactly what she was thinking. In a swift move, he lifted her into his arms and carried her back to the couch. He gently sat, placing her on his lap. The couch groaned under their weight, but that didn't stop the excitement growing inside her bosom.

Without waiting for him to make the move, Alexa pressed her lips to his to turn up the heat again between them. With her sitting on his lap as well and enjoying their passionate moment, could be very scandalous. But who was going to tell?

The last time she recalled sneaking around to kiss a beau was when she was courting Harrison, the boy who she thought she'd marry someday. But he was older and moved on to a woman who was ready for marriage.

A year later, her father convinced her to marry Jeffery, the son of a rancher who had his money at her father's bank. Reluctantly, she married him. It was difficult to marry someone she didn't love.

Jeffery left with his cousins to round up the cattle and move them from Denver to Boulder, Colorado, where they lived. Along the way, he contracted cholera from drinking water from a bad area. The disease took him quickly. She had been married for not quite three months. It wasn't even long enough to even consider herself married.

But the men she had met and stolen kisses from since then, did not compare to Ash. She sighed as she continued running her fingers through his hair. This moment could last forever as far as she was concerned.

There was no way he was the man called Hawk. He didn't have a rough bone in his body. In fact, he had been nothing but tender with her this entire time.

She shifted a bit on his lap, leaning back. Ash followed her down onto the couch, just as a loud crack sounded beneath them.

Ash ended their kiss rather quickly just as the back of the couch collapsed. He pushed her away and struggled to stand. She scrambled to her feet but slipped to the floor. The couch broke completely, sucking Ash into the hole in between the cushions.

The surprised look on his face was humorous. She burst out laughing.

"Are you hurt?" Ash squirmed in the crevice, trying to get out.

"No." Alexa kept laughing. "I'm sorry, you look so funny." She stood and extended her hand to assist in helping him up.

He took it and she pulled him off the couch. Ash brushed his pants to get the dust off. Glancing back at the broken couch, he shook his head and laughed.

"Well, I guess that ruined the mood," he said.

She touched her lips, feeling the puffiness of them. "It worked, though."

Moonstone and Mistrust

"What?"

"I'm not cold anymore." She grinned.

"Well, just let me know if that changes, because I know the cure." He wandered over to the saddlebag and pulled out a brown paper sack. "Are you hungry?"

"I suppose I can eat."

He handed her the bag so she could pick out her biscuit. It was too bad they weren't back at the ranch eating these. At least there she could find butter and honey.

Alexa put her hands on a wooden chair and shook it to make sure it was stable, then sat and pulled out a biscuit to eat. She handed the bag back to him. He leaned up against the wall and gazed at her. She needed to get him talking. More than anything, she needed to prove to herself that he wasn't the thief so she could scratch him from her list of suspects and consider him a possible romantic interest instead.

"So, tell me, Ash, what did you do in Utah before you left?" Alexa took a bite of her biscuit. His gaze moved from hers to the floor. He was obviously hiding something.

"That's a part of my life I'd like to forget," he replied. "I don't have many good memories."

"Then what about your family? Where are they living?" she asked. "Are they still in Utah?"

"I haven't seen them for many years. I'm afraid they are dead. I don't know of any other family around." He shook his head. "What about yours? Do you have siblings?"

"I have a younger brother. Do you have siblings?" She didn't want to talk about her family, she needed to know more about Ash's.

"No, I don't. So, you said your father is a banker. Will his promotion be in Colorado Springs or are you continuing onward after that?"

"Colorado Springs is where the bank is located." She nodded. That wasn't a lie. Her father's new bank was in Colorado Springs. "Have you been there?"

"I was there a few months ago," he replied. "Mr. O'Leary sends me there for supplies." He wandered to the window and looked out. "This snow is going to block the pass. We will need to return to the O'Leary ranch when we can." He faced her. "I'm sorry, Alexa, I really wanted you to find your family. I know what it's like to be lost without any relatives around. You see, I've been without my family for eighteen years." He sighed. "I feel I can tell you this. I was kidnapped from my home in Colorado when I was ten years old and taken to Utah and made to work in the mines for an evil woman. She told me that my family had died, and I needed to stay there. I believed her."

Alexa nearly lost her breath. *Finally!* He was talking about the mines, and those children kidnapped. Was he Hawk? Part of her didn't believe he was. Not any longer. After all, Hawk was a violent man, and Ash was so very kind and gentle.

"This was in the newspaper, wasn't it?" She stood and went to the window. "They caught the woman, right?"

"Yes. She was caught, along with the men who helped her. As I said, it's something I really want to remove from my mind. I wish it wouldn't have happened, but it did. I can't change the past."

"I heard that some of her righthand men were once prisoners. Is that true?" Her heart raced as she asked that important question. She was pretty sure he knew Hawk since he admitted to working in the mines.

He hesitated and his shoulders sagged. "Yes, some were."

"I can only imagine what that does to a person. I doubt they would be able to change their lives after all the bad things they had done, right?"

He moved away from the window quickly. Ash's footsteps were heavy. Had she hit a nerve with her questions?

"I would like to hope people can change," he replied. "God gives everyone a chance to redeem themselves. Even if we don't think we deserve it. I'm sure people will still mess up along the way, but as long as they keep trying to do better, God will understand."

Moonstone and Mistrust

"I'm sorry if I've said anything to offend you. Were you friends with some of the righthand men?" Alexa followed Ash near the fire.

"Yes. I made friends with many there. The only way to survive was to do as you were told."

Alexa looked back to the window. The snow was falling heavier, in large amounts. If they didn't return soon, they'd be snowed in here without many supplies.

"I think we should chance it and head back to the ranch before we are stuck here," she said. "This is probably the last snowstorm before spring arrives. These storms can last for days."

"I was just going to suggest that." He pulled a watch out of his pocket and flipped it open.

A shimmer from the watch caught her attention. The gold watch had gems on the front of the cover. She stepped closer to him.

"That's a nice watch," she replied.

"I thought so too." He closed it and handed it to her. "I've never seen anything like it before."

Alexa took the watch from his hand and studied it. She had seen this before. The front had an engraving of a bear on it with gems for the eyes.

Her heart began to sink deeper into her chest, causing a hollow feeling. This pocket watch was displayed in her father's bank. It was an heirloom that was carried across the Great Plains by her grandfather. Pa had put it in a display cabinet at the bank. It had been stolen along with many other items.

There was only one reason why Ash would have this. It was because he was the bank robber. He must be Hawk. What other excuse could there be?

Alexa's stomach twisted to where she felt like she wanted to gag. How could she let herself fall for him?

She quickly handed back the watch. "You'd better keep that safe. You wouldn't want someone to steal something so important."

"Maybe someday I'll turn it in for some money." He turned back to the fireplace and stirred it around to break up the small flames. "We don't have time to wait for the fire to die. It's small enough it shouldn't burn down the place when we leave."

Alexa pulled her jacket around her more, bracing for the cold blizzard that awaited her outside. As soon as she returned to the ranch, she would start hunting for more items. It bothered her knowing that he would carry a stolen item on his person. Not many people knew what the items looked like that were stolen. She had spent many days helping her father at the bank, so she knew what everything looked like.

It didn't take long for them to be saddled and on their way through the snow again. Ash put his horse in a faster trot, so she did the same. Getting home quickly was top priority. The temperatures were dropping fast.

After an hour of riding, the blizzard thinned out a bit to where she could see the Rocky Mountains. Suddenly, the painting from her father's office popped into her mind. That was the exact picture she saw at the O'Leary's home—another item stolen from the bank.

She shook her head in disbelief. It was staring her right in the face earlier and she didn't even recognize it.

Another memory opened in her mind. *The carousel.* Now she recalled why it was familiar and why she felt homesick when studying it. That too, had been in her father's bank.

Alexa gripped the reins harder as anger shot through her. It would be extremely difficult to act normally around the man who put her father out of business and crippled her brother.

No matter how handsome Ash was, he would pay for this. One way or another.

SIX

First thing this morning, after Alexa had dressed, she made her way toward the dining area. As she turned down a different hall, she studied the pictures hanging on the walls, or the trinkets displayed in a glass case, to see if any of them appeared familiar. Now that she realized Ash held one of the pieces from her father's bank, she suspected there would be more around the ranch. Although she didn't have a list of the items that were stolen from the bank, it would be easy to obtain since the sheriff had it. Of course, she would have to ride all the way back to Utah just to get it. Either that, or she would wire the sheriff's office and have them send it to her.

Paying more attention to trying to find more of the stolen items, she nearly missed the room leading inside the dining area. She stopped quickly and hurried inside...then stopped again. Ash and Mr. O'Leary were the only two sitting at the long table. From the sparce amount of food on their plates, she surmised they were finishing their breakfast.

When Ash's attention rested on her, his eyes widened, and he grinned. He took the linen napkin from his lap and wiped his mouth before standing. It took a few lagging seconds before the ranch owner remembered his manners when a lady entered a room and rose to his feet.

"Good morning," Ash said with a lift in his voice.

"Indeed, it's a wonderful day." She moved toward him but stopped at the end of the buffet-style table along the outside wall. The heavenly aroma of sausage, egg, and griddle cakes filled the air, making her stomach growl from hunger.

"I'm surprised you are up so early," Ash continued. "Especially after our um, *hectic* day yesterday."

"I usually awake with the sun." She gave him a sweet smile even if she couldn't feel the *sweet* emotion inside her. "Are you heading out on the ranch?"

"No. This morning Mr. O'Leary and I are riding into Erie. We've got a prospective buyer lined up for some horses." He paused and gently touched her arm. "I'm sure Mrs. O'Leary will keep you company while we're away."

"That's not necessary. I'm thinking of heading back into town to see if the sheriff or a Pinkerton agent has talked to my parents when they passed this way the other day." It was all she could do not to pull away from his touch. But she wasn't ready to explain to him why she didn't want to get personal with him now, especially when yesterday she felt completely opposite.

"Do you need someone to go with you?" Ash asked.

"No. I'll take my horse. We'll be fine now that it has stopped snowing."

"Well, if you need anything while I'm out, let Mrs. O'Leary know."

"Let's go," Mr. O'Leary snapped.

Ash's gaze jumped to the older man before returning to Alexa. "We should be back by noon."

"Have a safe journey."

"Will you meet me in Longmont for lunch when I return?" Ash asked.

Her heartbeat quickened. "Absolutely. I shall meet you there."

She finally moved out of his reach and stepped closer toward the food. She waited until the men were out of the room before turning and picking up a plate. She piled the food on quickly, then sat at the table and ate. Although she tried not to eat like a person starved to death, she couldn't get enough. It had been a while since she tasted food this delicious.

"I see you are enjoying the morning meal."

The woman's voice behind Alexa made her jump and turn toward the other person in the room, walking in from the adjoining door. This must be the cook Ash had mentioned. The round woman wore a white apron around her thick waist with a smudge of flour on her chin and cheek.

Alexa wiped her mouth with the linen napkin and shifted in her chair to see the cook better. "Yes, the food is very tasty. Did you make it?"

The woman's aged eyes sparkled, and she smiled. "I've been cooking for the O'Learys since before the ranch became profitable." She slid her palm along the tight bun holding her white hair in place. "I've been very happy here."

That was difficult to believe, especially since Alexa found the O'Learys to be an odd couple who were not very sociable. Either that or Alexa was overly suspicious.

"I'm sure the ranch hands love you to pieces." Alexa chuckled. "Most men don't get fed this well."

The cook nodded toward Alexa's mostly empty plate. "It appears you don't get fed well, either."

Embarrassment climbed up Alexa's face, heating her. The cook was correct. In Alexa's line of work, eating food this good was a treat.

"Traveling so often makes me wish for my home where there is a kitchen. I do hope to settle down soon." She wiped the corners of her mouth. "When did the ranch become profitable?"

"About five years ago. Mr. O'Leary has a good eye for potential buyers. Selling and breeding his horses had been his dream. Many people have graciously helped him out."

"The furnishings in the home are so beautiful. Wherever did he find these paintings and artifacts? I've been admiring them since I arrived."

"They have been collecting them over the years. Sometimes I've seen him come in with armfuls of new items." The cook brushed her hands on the apron. "He enjoys taking Hawk with him when he goes out."

The piece of bacon that she held between her fingers broke in half as it dropped from her grip. *Hawk*. Alexa's heart raced. She gulped slowly not to give away her cover.

"Hawk? He has a bird?" Alexa acted innocently.

The woman chuckled, making her round face turn red. The cook shook her head. "Oh, no. Hawk is a man. He was just here having breakfast with Mr. O'Leary."

"Ash?" Alexa's throat grew dry. She didn't want to hear that they were the same person, but the pain in her heart was telling her they were.

"Yes. Ash Hawk." The cook smiled. "He has such lovely green eyes."

Alexa's hands nervously shook, and she quickly placed them in her lap. Suddenly, she wasn't hungry any longer. The sooner she got him behind bars the better.

Why had she crossed that line she promised herself never to go near? She had vowed never to fall for a criminal. Yet, the kiss they shared had changed her mind. Her first instincts had been correct about Ash—Hawk. So, how had she let his charm sway her?

"Indeed, he has nice eyes." Alexa swallowed to moisten her dry throat. She looked down at her plate. "Oh, I think my eyes are bigger than my stomach. I can't eat another bite."

"Well, I'd better get back to cleaning the kitchen and preparing the chow for lunch." She nodded at Alexa. "Have a nice day."

"Thank you."

Alexa watched the woman head back through the swinging doors. Anger welled inside her and she bunched her hands into fists. Why did the thief have to be Ash? He had hurt her brother during a robbery. Yet, what she had gotten to know about Ash led her to believe he was a kind man. It was going to be a struggle taking him to jail, but she would feel so much better knowing justice was served.

Her gaze moved about the dining room. Shelves stacked on the west wall holding empty glass jars in odd-looking shapes. They were most likely collectibles since nothing was stored inside. She looked up to the top shelf to a lovely porcelain carousel.

Alexa gasped. That was in her father's bank, too! She recalled it had been one of her favorite things to look at when she visited him while he worked.

She reached into her pocket and pulled out her little notepad and pencil. Keeping a log of these items would prove to be beneficial. Marking their whereabouts would make it easier for the authorities to confiscate them and return them to the rightful owners.

Once she wrote it down, she slid them back into her pocket. She picked up her plate and walked to the garbage pail to toss the uneaten food. She hadn't lied. After realizing Hawk was the one she'd kissed passionately, she had lost her appetite.

Alexa needed to ride into town to visit the Pinkerton Office in Longmont before noon. She wanted to make certain she was finished with her business before Ash sauntered back into town. Acting friendly toward Ash would be difficult, but she could do it. Putting on an act was all part of being a Pinkerton agent.

She heard through the grapevine that the famous Pinkerton agent, Dusty Sloan, managed the office in town. His great reputation for being a detective was another reason she needed to meet with him. He brought down a diamond theft all within a few weeks. Of course, he had some help from his future wife. Alexa couldn't wait to meet him in person. Agent Sloan would understand her desire to become an agent. She knew he'd hire her once he had seen how she single-handedly brought in the infamous *Hawk*.

Just thinking of his name sent exciting chills over her body. His warm lips touching hers made her feel at home. Ash's arms were strong, and tingles danced on her lower back where they were yesterday during their embrace. *Stop it!*

Ash Hawk was a thief. There was no way she would give her heart to a criminal.

* * * *

Longmont, Colorado was bustling with people. It was almost as busy as Boulder. Tall trees lined sections of the street. Alexa rode past the newly built white brick building for the Colorado Bank and Trust. Hopefully this town was luckier than Salt Lake City, and not have their bank robbed.

Across from the bank, a smaller brown brick building sat nestled between two other structures. One which was the sheriff's office. Alexa dismounted and wrapped the reins around the hitching post. She smoothed out her dress and adjusted her red hat that she wore and headed toward the Pinkerton office.

She twisted the handle, pushed the door open, and stepped inside. Three desks sat in the spacious room, two agents sat behind their hard wooden desks, helping other people. Hanging on the walls were awards complimenting the Pinkertons.

From the desk toward the back, she noticed an older couple standing in front as they talked to the agent. The older gentleman had his arm wrapped around the woman in a consoling way.

"Agent Sloan? Are you certain our son wasn't one of those missing children?" the woman's voice asked in desperation.

"It has been months since those missing children were released from the mines in Salt Lake City. We want to think our son is still alive," the man said, squeezing his wife's shoulder.

Alexa's interest grew. They were discussing the same mines that Hawk had been working at. Their child must have gone missing years ago. How terrible it would be to lose someone so young. They were most likely convinced their child was dead, and then they must have read about how all the children were rescued. Of course, they would want confirmation. If she were a Pinkerton, she'd have their answer.

"I have asked for the list of names," the agent replied in a deep voice.

She dropped her gaze to the name plaque on his desk. *Agent Dusty Sloan.* Her heart skipped a beat. Here was the very man she wanted to meet—and convince him that he should make her an agent because she was going to bring in Ash Hawk.

"I'm sure you realize," Agent Sloan continued, "that many families are searching for their missing children. But rest assured, we will find them all." He pointed to a paper on the desk. "I'm taking names of all the families who have come seeking our help. Will you tell me your name?"

"Of course." The older man squared his shoulders. "I'm Leo Hawkins—"

"Excuse me." Another voice pulled her away from the conversation she had been eavesdropping on. "May I help you?"

Alexa faced a man who had walked up behind her. He had dark blond hair, combed very stylish away from his face. A small mustache rested above his lip. His eyes were as blue as the ocean that she remembered seeing as a child. The man's broad shoulders filled out his brown suit coat, and he stood at least as tall as Ash, which was over six feet tall. He was as attractive as Ash... Well, almost.

"Good morning." She held out her hand. "My name is Alexa Moore. I need to speak with Agent Sloan."

The man shook her hand, and warmth spread throughout her body. He looked over her shoulder toward the other agent's desk. The other couple were still talking to Agent Sloan.

The man's gaze landed back on hers. His eyes were nearly as breathtaking as Ash's. Inwardly, she seethed. She really needed to stop thinking of *him* that way.

"Agent Sloan is busy. But can I help you instead? I'm Agent Montgomery." He gave her a wink. "You may call me Levi, if you'd like."

"Oh." Her cheeks warmed up from his flirtation. "I don't know if you can help."

"Give me a try."

She wasn't sure about his wording. Was he still flirting? "Well, you see, I have some valuable information, but I'll only exchange it for a promise."

"A promise?" His eyes narrowed in confusion.

"I want to be a Pinkerton agent." Alexa stood taller as she spoke, determined to show him her boldness. She was tired of taking *no* for an answer. She would fight them this time.

Agent Montgomery casually folded his arms. His gaze moved slowly over her body as if he liked what he saw. Of course, today she looked more like a lady than her usual attire.

Alexa found this type of attention rather exciting, yet very improper. Her mind drifted to Ash who had done that to her on many occasions since they met. It thrilled her to know Ash liked what he saw, but was Agent Montgomery measuring her up to the other agents, or was he admiring what he saw, too?

"Miss Moore," Levi's voice was soothing. "I hate to tell you this, but we do not send attractive young ladies out into the world to hunt down criminals. Mr. Pinkerton has indeed used a few older women to befriend the women who are close to the criminals, but it takes a certain type of woman to do that. You, Miss Moore, appear to be very delicate, like a rose. Maybe Agent Sloan can hire you as a clerk here in this office."

Alexa stepped forward, standing almost nose to nose with Levi. His cologne smelled wonderful.

"Agent Montgomery. Do not judge a book by its cover." She arched an eyebrow, challenging him. "I have single-handedly brought criminals to local sheriffs from Utah to Colorado—not once, but several times. I can give you the names and locations of these sheriffs to confirm my story. I am not afraid to get dirty. Staying up all night and sleeping in the mountains is not a problem for me. And if you must know, underneath this dress is no petticoat, but men's trousers."

His eyes widened and a small grin stretched across his face. "Miss Moore, I'm sorry to say, but we don't hire young, single women. However, I do like your spunk."

"I am a widow, if you must know." She stepped back and folded her arms. "I've been a widow now for five years."

"Oh." His eyes widened again. "And you are still unmarried?"

"I am. As I said, don't judge a book by its cover. There are many things I can do that would surprise you, Agent Sloan... and Mr. Pinkerton."

Agent Montgomery motioned his hand for her to sit on the chair by his desk. She hesitated, then followed him, pausing to look in Agent Sloan's direction. The older couple were still talking to him about their missing son.

"I'm very intrigued, Miss Moore," Levi said. "Please, sit down."

"I really need to speak with Agent Sloan." She looked again at the door. "That is Agent Dusty Sloan, right?"

"Agent Sloan is busy, as you can see. This couple had been waiting for him for days. Their son was kidnapped years ago and they need closure. Their boy is dead. They just can't accept it." He sat down.

Alexa sat across from him. "Do they have proof he is deceased?"

"No, Miss Moore. But he's been gone for quite some time. A child's bones were found in the Grand Canyon area. We are convinced that they belong to the missing boy. But enough about that. Before we continue, I have a question for you."

"All right."

"If you are widowed, why do you call yourself *Miss* Moore? Shouldn't it be *Mrs.* Moore?"

She chuckled. "Levi, you are the one who referred to me as *Miss*, not I. But if you require proof of my status, I can show you a marriage certificate and my husband's death certificate."

His shoulder relaxed and he shook his head. "I don't require proof. So, tell me what information you have for Agent Sloan."

"Are you familiar with the notorious bank robber Hawk?"

His eyes rounded wider. "I am."

"I know where he is, and I'm willing to exchange this information for a job as a Pinkerton agent." Alexa smiled. "And I will not give you Hawk's whereabouts until you, Agent Sloan, or Mr. Pinkerton himself can assure me of a position as an agent." She would not give in this time.

51

SEVEN

Alexa studied Levi Montgomery closely, hoping to see a light of awareness in his lovely blue eyes, or at least a hint that he was taking her deal into consideration. He took his finger and smoothed it across his mustache.

"You know where the bank robber is?" Levi asked.

"Yes. I've been hot on his trail for a while now."

"And he doesn't suspect you are after him?" Levi picked up his pencil and twirled it between his fingers. "You do know that if you are hiding him from the authorities, you can be punished as well."

"I'm not hiding him. I'm... well, I'm currently working undercover. That is all I can tell you until I am promised the position as a Pinkerton agent."

"I would need to discuss this with Agent Sloan. He is a very busy man. It may take a while."

Alexa received the impression that Levi was stalling. Maybe she should just push her way into Agent Sloan's office and lay her offer on the table. Levi acted as though he didn't fully believe her.

He stopped the pencil from twirling between his fingers as his eyes narrowed on her.

She lifted her chin, keeping her determination. "How about I give you a day to discuss this matter with Agent Sloan, Agent Montgomery? I shall return to town tomorrow to see how badly you want your notorious bank robber behind bars."

"And if I get your answer sooner, how do I find you?" His blue eyes darkened a little as a grin stretched across his face.

"As I said, I'm undercover. I can't reveal my secrets to anyone yet. All you need to know is I'm looking for my missing family." Alexa stood and stretched her hand out. "Good day, Agent Montgomery. I hope to hear from you really soon."

Levi stood and took her hand into his, but instead of shaking it, he brought her knuckles to his lips and brushed a soft kiss across her skin. She found his gesture very bold, even though she thought it was romantic. Her heart fluttered a little.

"I will be waiting for your return," Levi replied. "Let me walk you to the door."

Alexa followed him to the door. "I'm quite serious about my offer, and I'm not one to be trifled with."

"May I ask one thing?" He opened the door for her. "Why do you want to be a Pinkerton agent?"

Although she had given this excuse to other agents in Utah, she hoped one of them would take her seriously for once. "I want to live in a place where I don't fear for my life or the lives of others. When people are hurt or victimized, justice must be served. For instance, all those children who were kidnapped years ago in Utah, why did it take so long for them to be found? I know there were a few lately that made the front page of the newspaper for helping to solve the crime, but they had been missing for years. I believe more agents would have been able to bring those children home safely." Alexa stepped past Levi, turned, and cordially smiled. "I want to be one who helps keep others safe, and whether I'm a Pinkerton agent or not, I will continue to help the community. Having me work with you will only benefit the agency." She squared her shoulders. "Good day, Agent Montgomery."

She stepped onto the wooden walk and continued on her way. A slight frustration built inside her chest. Agent Sloan would have understood her need, not Agent Blue Eyes.

Moving her fingers to her lips, she touched them softly. Not often had she experienced a man's kiss, and although Agent Montgomery's lips were gentle against her knuckles, it was Ash's kiss that had left a deep impression on her. Butterflies danced in her stomach as she thought about him, yet she needed to face that truth. Ash was a thief. He might not be a kidnapper anymore, but his life was molded into doing evil things.

To take her mind off her mixed feelings for him, Alexa decided to go into the hat shop and try on some new bonnets to pass the time. She really wanted to return to the ranch to take more inventory and sneak around and look for places Ash would hide his loot. But since she agreed to meet up with him in town for lunch, she needed to keep up her ruse. If he knew she suspected him, he would make a run for it. She wasn't about to let that happen.

Alexa tightened a red lady's hat over her head. The style of bonnets was certainly changing, and she loved how these new styles looked on her. Of course, red had always seemed to bring out the feistiness in her. As she stared at herself in the mirror, she wondered if her tactics were convincing enough. The way Levi Montgomery looked at her made her believe he didn't think she could pull off being a spy.

She turned her head to one side and batted her eyes. Levi would not put words into her mind to discourage her from her dreams. She could do this. She had been capturing outlaws for the local sheriffs for a few years already. Indeed, she was good enough to be a Pinkerton agent.

Alexa carried the hat up to the counter to pay for it. Hanging on the wall behind the clerk was a small golden clock with a revolving bottom. Immediately, recognition struck. This was another missing piece from her father's bank. But what was it doing here?

"Will this be all?" the brunette woman asked. The woman was probably around Alexa's age, maybe a few years older.

"Yes, thank you." Alexa pulled out the dollars from her coin purse. "May I say what a beautiful clock you have." She pointed toward the wall. "Wherever did you purchase it? I would love one for my home."

The woman glanced behind her at the clock. "Oh, this?" She chuckled. "It is indeed a lovely clock. It was given to us as a barter to purchase a few hats."

"Hats, you say?" Alexa wondered why Ash would use trinkets to exchange with instead of the money he had stolen. The woman nodded. "Yes, hats. I know it is hard to believe, but I swear that is exactly what happened."

"Well, it's lovely. I remember seeing one similar in Utah."

The clerk's eyebrows arched. "I wonder if the clockmaker lived there." She placed Alexa's hat inside a box and handed it to her.

"By chance, do you remember who used it to barter?" Alexa asked innocently as she ran her fingers over the package.

The woman pulled out a book from under the counter and flipped a few pages back. "Oh, yes, here it is, the name was Ash Hawk."

Bile built up in Alexa's throat again. That was not the name she wanted to hear, even though she knew it was him. She swallowed hard, trying not to lose what was in her stomach.

"Thank you. I would have to find this person to get more information on where the clock was purchased. Have a good day." Alexa forced a smile and quickly exited the store.

The town seemed to have more people wandering about the streets now than when she first arrived. She glanced in all directions, trying to decide which road Ash would be coming from. The time was nearing noon. A diner across the street was nestled between a bakery and a barbershop, making it the perfect place for their lunch.

After looking both ways, she led her horse across the street to the diner and tied the animal up on the hitching post. She petted Pegasus' snout, and her horse neighed softly.

"What shall I do, Pegasus?" she whispered, leaning her head against the horse. "I don't know if I'm strong enough to keep pretending."

"Miss Moore," the deep voice of Agent Montgomery tickled her ears. She whipped around and faced him.

"Are you by chance following me? Or perhaps you are a mind reader." He winked as he stepped closer. "But since you are at my favorite diner, would you care to have lunch with me?"

"Agent Montgomery." She swallowed hard. Alexa didn't expect to see him so soon. "I didn't see you come over."

"Of course not, since you were comforting your horse. Is the animal ill?" Levi placed his hand on Pegasus' neck. "She feels fine."

"I was just reassuring her that we would be heading home soon." She wasn't about to tell him her thoughts of doubt.

"Home? I haven't seen you around town. Did you recently move here?" His hand continued stroking the horse's mane.

"I'm passing through. I became lost and found shelter before the storm hit at the O'Leary's Ranch." Alexa figured that would be fine to say. She wasn't giving any hint as to where Hawk was hiding. Yet, it seemed strange, Hawk wasn't really hiding. Did he not think anyone would recognize him?

"Gunther and Rosanna O'Leary?" Levi arched his eyebrows. "They usually don't take in outsiders, unless you are working on their ranch."

"I suppose they had no choice." Alexa shrugged. "Their ranch hands brought me in as the storm was approaching."

"So, do you often travel by yourself? Because that is very dangerous."

"Did you forget, Agent Montgomery, I did say I knew how to take care of myself?" She brushed her hands down her brown skirt to remove some dust that had settled on it.

His gaze wandered over her again. It should have made her uncomfortable, but instead she quite enjoyed the attention. He was welcome to look all he wanted, just as long as he was able to make her a Pinkerton agent.

"Will you join me for lunch?" he asked.

"Did you talk with Agent Sloan?" Alexa quickly changed the subject.

He grinned. "I did, and he suggested that you apply for the secretary position. So, how about that lunch?"

"I am very sorry to say, Agent Montgomery, but I am waiting for someone, and we will have lunch here."

Levi's grin slowly diminished. "You don't say?"

"He has promised me that he will help me find my family." Alexa decided to continue with this ruse. Levi didn't need to know that she had lied about that particular aspect of her ruse.

"One of the ranch hands?" he asked. "You should be wary of them. Not many can be trusted. They are drifters. Some might take advantage of a sweet lady, as yourself."

Sadly, she didn't trust anyone. Not anymore.

"I will be cautious." Alexa nodded. "Thank you for your concern."

From the corner of her eye, she saw the front door to the Pinkerton office open and a tall man, with broad shoulders and wearing a black duster, stepped out. Her heart skipped a beat. It was Dusty Sloan. He put a black cowboy hat on top of his head as he looked around. His gaze landed on hers, then moved to Levi's. Taking large swift steps, he hurried across the street.

"Agent Montgomery." Dusty's voice was very authoritative sounding. "Pardon me, ma'am." He tipped his hat to her then looked back to Levi. "I just received a telegram that a bank was robbed in Erie. We need to go immediately."

Alexa's hopes dropped as her heart shattered again. Ash was in Erie this morning with Mr. O'Leary. She had wondered if the two men had been working together. The news from Agent Sloan confirmed her doubts. Ash was indeed the infamous bank robber, Hawk.

She bunched her hands into fists. If Dusty and Levi caught Ash, that would leave her with nothing. There would be no leverage to become a Pinkerton agent.

"I will meet up with you later, Miss Moore." Levi tipped his cream-colored hat.

Deep inside, she wanted to scream. She wanted to beg them to let her go with them, but she knew they wouldn't allow it. Alexa tried not to let her expression show the dejection she felt that they were leaving without her. As she watched the two men hurry across the street, from the opposite end of town her focus landed on a lone rider coming toward her.

Ash. He had been watching her conversation with Levi, she was certain of it. As he neared, she quickly looked toward Levi and Dusty as they mounted their steeds and took off riding fast through town, stirring up plenty of dust.

Alexa's gaze jumped back to Ash's. He dismounted and tied his horse next to Pegasus. Her heart thumped quickly.

"Alexa," he began. "Did the Pinkertons find your family?"

She let out a slow breath. "No. But they are going to keep their eyes open and ask around for me."

Ash frowned. "I feel terrible that I wasn't able to get you through the pass before the snowstorm hit. If I would have been quicker, maybe you would be with your family now."

"Nonsense." She reached out and touched his arm. "You shouldn't feel bad." She paused, trying to think of something clever to say so he wouldn't doubt her cover. "Besides, you saved me in another way." She grinned.

"Another way?" His green eyes twinkled as he stepped closer.

"You kept me from freezing to death." Her heart hammered hard, feeling like that particular organ in her chest would jump right out.

Why did she wish to be in his arms again? *No, no, no!* She needed to be strong. This man hurt her brother and she would make sure he paid for his crimes. Besides, Levi seemed interested in her. But giving her heart to any man right now was very dangerous.

EIGHT

Watching Alexa talking with that Pinkerton agent left a sour feeling in Ash's stomach. From his observation, that man was flirting with Alexa, and it seemed as though she accepted his advances. Of course, she would want another man. Ash had nothing to offer her. Absolutely nothing. He certainly didn't have a great job, and he wasn't sure when he would get his own home. A woman like Alexa needed more.

However, since she brought up the enjoyable moment they shared in the cabin, maybe he just read her wrong. All morning long, he dreamed of holding her in his arms again and tasting her sweet lips. Butterflies danced in his stomach. Just thinking about it made him happy.

"Oh, this place is quite busy," Alexa commented as they entered the diner.

"It is the only diner in town. They are pretty quick, though. The other ranch hands brought me here on my birthday." Ash walked with Alexa to a table, and he pulled out a chair for her. She smiled and sat.

"It smells wonderful," she said.

"Their food is decent. The O'Leary's cook is the best, though. No one tops her."

"I had a chat with her this morning." Alexa's cheerful expression faded slightly. "She mentioned someone named Hawk. Do you know who she is talking about?" Her eyes blinked a few times as she looked at him.

"That is me," Ash replied. "Ash Hawk. May I ask what she said about me?"

Alexa's pause seemed to be longer than normal. That made him a little anxious, because he couldn't tell if she was happy about hearing his name or not.

"She said you have lovely green eyes." Alexa smiled. "I agree. Your eyes look like emeralds at times."

He reached across the table and touched her hand. She immediately stiffened. Did she do that because they were in public? Perhaps he had been too bold. He wasn't sure how to be a true gentleman, even though he wanted to be.

"People have told me that my eyes turn darker when I'm feeling emotional." He ran his thumb across her stiff knuckles. "Like when I get caught up in desire."

Her throat jumped as what must have been a hard swallow. Ash grinned, knowing he brought her thoughts back to their kiss. Slowly, her hand relaxed. He knew he should be careful with his affection toward her in public. Ruining her reputation in any way was something he never wanted to do.

"Well, your eyes are lovely either way," she told him. "The cook also said many of the other ranch hands look up to you."

"We all work together pretty well, I suppose." Ash shrugged. "When I was in the mines, that was how we got through the day. We helped each other to make the load lighter."

"Can I ask you a question?"

"Of course, Alexa."

"Don't be angry at me for asking this, but you knew it was wrong to kidnap those children, right?" Alexa's voice shook as she spoke.

"I didn't take them." Ash leaned over the table, keeping his voice low. "Big Ed had others who did that. My job was to keep them from leaving the mine. I had to keep reminding them that their parents were dead." Ash's voice cracked. It was a terrible thing to do, but that was what happened to him when he had been kidnapped. All he did was treat the newly kidnapped children as he had been treated. "I didn't know any better. Besides, Big Ed threatened me, and the others. I did what I needed to do to survive."

Moonstone and Mistrust

Alexa's hand slid out from under his and she placed it on top of his and patted it softly. Her expression relaxed.

"I'm sorry for asking that. I just wanted to make sure you knew right from wrong," she said.

"Yes, I do." Even though she seemed a little more at ease with him, he wished he had never told her about his time in the mines. He had hated every minute of it. It was torture most of his life. It bothered him knowing what he had done. Yet one thing he remembered his friend, Ben, telling him in the mines, was never give up on God. There was a plan for everything. God would help them survive as long as they kept praying.

It was still difficult to forgive himself for not standing up for those children. Ash constantly lied to them. Bowser instructed Ash to convince the children they had a different last name, just in case one of them was fortunate enough to run away a few years after working in the mines. It was difficult not to wonder if that was what happened to him. Yet Hawk was the only name he remembered, so they must not have brainwashed him. Sadly, he would always feel the burden of guilt for not trying to change things earlier in his life.

He shook his head slightly, hoping to get the bad memories out of his mind. As long as Alexa liked him regardless of his faults, that was all that mattered.

"So, what is good to eat here?" Alexa asked.

"They make a very good turkey sandwich," he replied. "They also have tasty soups. Chili and cornbread are probably their most popular dish, though."

"I think soup sounds wonderful on this cool day."

Ash lifted his hand to the waitress to come over. It was a good thing Mr. O'Leary paid him today, otherwise, he would be tight on money. Sitting across from Alexa was so refreshing. At times, her stare would seem confused as if she were in deep thought. He was pretty sure she was worried about her family. As soon as that pass cleared, he would help her find them because he never backed down on a promise.

After lunch and on their ride home, Alexa didn't seem too talkative. Ash figured it had to be about not receiving the help she needed in town from the Pinkertons. Her family would be looking for her, he knew it. She had only been gone a few days, and they were most likely waiting for her on the other side of Granger Pass.

Ash left Alexa at O'Leary's ranch while he rode out to the road that led to the pass. A small avalanche this morning slid down the mountain, covering the road, making it impossible to travel through.

Just as he had suspected, no one was even out there trying to dig it away. They would have to wait until spring arrived and the rain and sun melted it, which could easily be another few weeks away.

He grinned. More time to spend with Alexa. He just hoped she saw it that way.

By the time he made it back to the ranch, it was dinner time. He quickly washed up so he could sit by Alexa during the meal. He wished he had more time to clean up after the ride, but his growling stomach told him he could wait.

He stepped into the dining room and glanced at the long table. The ranch hands were already digging into their stew that the cook had prepared. His gaze wandered around the table looking for Alexa, but she wasn't there. How odd. He figured she would have helped the cook again.

Ash scooped up his stew and sat near the end of the table, leaving an open place for Alexa to sit when she arrived. Spoons clanked against the bowls as the men ate. Ash kept eyeing the door, waiting for her to come and eat.

"Where is that lady?" Johnny asked Ash after shoveling a spoonful of stew into his mouth. "Did you leave her in town?"

"Nah, I seen her earlier," Frankie replied. "She was readin' a book. I always wonder why women waste their time on readin'. Ain't gonna make her smarter than us."

Ash grunted as he took a bite. Alexa was the smartest woman he had ever met. From their conversation at lunchtime, he discovered that she was very knowledgeable of the trails.

Moonstone and Mistrust

Frankie was the one who needed to read more. While Ash was in the mines, Bowser read to them almost every day. Ash's favorite book was The Adventures of Tom Sawyer. Bowser even helped Ash practice reading so he could read to the children when they arrived.

"Miss Alexa said she wasn't feeling well," Mrs. O'Leary replied. "She went to bed early." Her gaze rested on Ash. "We aren't a hotel, Hawk. She needs to either find something to do to help on the ranch, or you need to take her to the Lonestar Hotel for her to take up residence."

"Yes, ma'am. I'm sure she will help here. If the cook doesn't need help, then I'll find something for her to do on the ranch."

"She asks too many questions." Mrs. O'Leary reached for a biscuit. "I'm not so sure why she is so concerned about the paintings hanging on the walls, and vases in my sitting room."

Ash shrugged. "Maybe she enjoys art."

"Well, she makes me nervous." Mrs. O'Leary shoved half of the biscuit into her mouth. "I don't trust people who ask too many questions."

He didn't think Alexa asked too many questions. He enjoyed hearing her talk. Whether it was because she had the sweetest voice he had ever heard or if it was because he liked the way her lips moved, he didn't know. Her laugh was delightful, and her kisses were heavenly.

Another tingle of excitement welled up in his stomach just thinking about her. If she hadn't run off so quickly when they got home from town, he would have tried to kiss her again.

After finishing the meal, the men all adjourned to the sitting room to play cards. Now would be the perfect time to sneak away to Alexa's room to check on her—as long as the other men didn't see him.

Ash grabbed a bowl and put some stew in it. Maybe she was hungry now. This would give him the perfect excuse to see her again. He hoped he would be able to convince her to go for a walk with him. Then, maybe he was just looking for an excuse to kiss her again. After all, he couldn't stop thinking about it.

Before leaving the kitchen, he noticed on the top shelf the porcelain carousel was gone. He looked around the room, wondering if it had been placed somewhere else. Ash couldn't see it. He knew that particular piece was quite expensive. Mr. O'Leary told him it was at least one hundred dollars.

With the bowl still in his hands, he headed up the servant stairs in the back of the house. The O'Leary's let the ranch hands relax in the main house, just so they would feel like a family. Many times he had explored this big home and knew where the secret places to hide were located.

He turned a corner and stopped in front of the guest room. Ash tapped softly on the door, just in case Alexa had a headache. He leaned his ear closer to the door to listen for movements. There weren't any. He tapped again, but harder this time.

"Alexa," he called out. "It's Ash. I brought you some stew."

He waited. Still no answer. Fear crept inside him. He knew Mr. O'Leary didn't care for Alexa, but he hoped he hadn't done anything to upset her. Out of instinct, he quickly opened the door. It was dark inside, but he could see the bed from the lanterns in the hallway. Her bed was empty.

Ash set the food down on the table and lit the candle until it brightened the room. Alexa's things were still there, so she hadn't been tossed out by Mrs. O'Leary yet. On the table was a notepad. He shouldn't look at it since it was probably personal to Alexa. Yet there was so much he still didn't know about her. Could she be hiding something? After all, Big Ed had seemed nice at first but turned out to be a very greedy and ruthless woman.

His hand touched the paper, but he hesitated to read. This was wrong. He shouldn't look, but curiosity won. And he focused on what was written. Alexa's perfect-looking handwriting covered the page in what appeared to be a list.

Mountain Painting – hanging on the wall in sitting room
Glass Angels – Mr. O'Leary's den
Soldier statues – Mr. O'Leary's den
Porcelain Carousal – kitchen shelf

Moonstone and Mistrust

Pocket Watch – Ash
Silver goblets – Mrs. O'Leary's China cabinet

Ash quickly straightened. Why was she writing about items in the O'Leary's home? And why was she concerned about his pocket watch? He pulled out the watch from his trousers and checked the time. It was nearing eight o'clock.

If she was snooping around the home and taking inventory of the O'Leary's possessions and got caught, he wasn't sure he would be able to save her this time. Mr. O'Leary would have the sheriff fetched posthaste.

Ash needed to find Alexa, and fast.

NINE

Alexa couldn't believe how messy some of these ranch hands were. Their beds were unmade, and dirty clothes scattered about their rooms. She had counted ten beds in the main room, and two more beds in a separate corner near the back door.

She knew dinner would be the best time to snoop while the men were eating. Alexa also knew Ash would be in the dining room, too. That would give her a chance to search through his things to find more missing items from her father's bank. Earlier in the afternoon, she noticed that the carousel in the kitchen was missing. Alexa needed to find that item. All of the stolen pieces needed to be located, and she had a feeling they were in this room.

Considering Mr. O'Leary had accompanied Ash to Erie where the bank was robbed, that put Mr. O'Leary on her suspect list as well. How could they not be working together on these heists? It was no wonder there were so many mixed descriptions of *Hawk*. It was because some people were describing Mr. O'Leary. Most criminals—whether bank or train robbers, or even jewel thieves—they all seemed to be in a gang of some type, and she was going to take down every last one of them.

Over the past twenty minutes, she had gone through all the drawers by each of the beds. Nothing looked out of the ordinary, and most of all, there wasn't anything that gave evidence Ash slept here. She didn't find any personal items, which confused her more. If this was where these men lived, why wouldn't they have anything personal? It would certainly make her job easier. But there was no more time today to snoop. The men would be finished with the meal and return to their beds soon.

There were only two more beds to search around, so she must hurry. She moved to the back two beds, which surprisingly were much neater than the others. She opened one of the drawers. Inside was long underwear, a couple of shirts, and a pistol. Loose coins lay in the back of the drawer.

She leaned closer and sniffed. There was a small hint in the air of Ash's scent from when she had been in his arms yesterday. Just as before, butterflies danced in her belly. She cursed her body for doing that, and wished she knew how to remove those feelings. If only she wouldn't think of him like that anymore.

Just to be sure this was Ash's spot, she crouched to look under the bed, hoping to recognize anything he'd had on his person when they had been together. A carpetbag was shoved near the head of the bed, so she reached underneath and gently tugged on it. There was something heavy inside of it.

Her heart pattered with excitement, thinking she might have just found some of the stolen items. *Yes, Ash Hawk you are going to jail for good.* As soon as those words escaped her thoughts, an uneasy feeling twisted in her gut.

Why was doubt sneaking in her head? She had been tracking him for quite some time. She had studied his habits from the information she had gathered on him, anyway. Yet why did she suddenly feel that something was wrong in this whole scenario? If only she knew why. Was it his kiss that made her question her own research?

"What are you doing here, Alexa?"

Ash's voice made her jump. Her blood turned to ice as fear ran through her.

She yanked her hand back, thinking of what to say to get out of this. Only one thing came to mind, and she quickly unhooked the watch around her wrist. She swung around and faced the man.

"Ash," she gasped, placing her hand on her heart. "You frightened me."

"Why are you in the men's bunk area?" He stepped closer to the bed. "And what are you doing on the floor?"

She dropped her gaze to the ground. "Oh, here it is." She picked up the watch and laughed. "You see, I came in here to wait for you." Alexa stood, fastening the watch back around her wrist. "You were taking too long, and... um, I got bored and was playing with my watch. It fell out of my hands. I thought I lost it."

She forced herself to smile even though she lied to him. She hated being dishonest, especially to Ash. The way he studied her, she was sure his mind was turning with doubt and whether or not he should believe her.

"But why are you here... in the sleeping quarters?" Again, he stepped even closer to her. His brow was wrinkled in confusion.

Think, Alexa! The only thing that came to her mind was their kiss. Oh, why did it have to be that?

"I... I just wanted to be alone with you for a moment." She swallowed hard.

"You do know if we are caught here, we could both get into trouble? Not only that, but your reputation would also be ruined." He looked around. "I'm surprised you were able to get in here without anyone seeing."

"Everyone was hungry." Her stomach rumbled slightly with the mention of food.

"Mrs. O'Leary said you had a headache. Are you feeling well?" Ash shifted on his feet.

"It was just an excuse so I could come look for you." It took all her might, but she stepped toward him, trying to act normal. "I hope you don't mind that I'm here."

"I'm just glad I found you and not one of the other men. Who knows what they would do to you." His gaze roamed over her slowly. "I can guarantee that they wouldn't act like a gentleman."

Alexa's heart pounded like a drum in a parade. She was sure Ash could hear it. She swallowed again.

"I don't want to think about that. I only want to know what you are going to do." She gazed into his green eyes, watching them turn darker by the second. "Ash, I want you to kiss me again."

Ash pulled her into his arms. Wasting no time, his lips blended with hers. The room felt like it was spinning, and her feet didn't feel as though they were touching the ground. She moved her arms around his neck, bringing back all the excitement from the cabin. His closeness made it difficult for her to catch her breath, but she loved it.

Feeling his hands roaming around her back sent tingles throughout her body. Then reality stepped in, and everything came to a screeching halt, pushing her emotions aside. She was kissing a bank robber, a thief, a man who didn't care to go around the poor child who stood in the road and hit him with his horse—like her brother.

Her body stiffened and she quickly broke the passionate kiss. She couldn't look at him. If she did, she would want to slap him, hog-tie him, and take him to the sheriff's office.

Alexa turned away to get her breathing under control. Ash touched her hair with his warm hands, sending a shiver down her spine.

"I'm sorry for being so bold," Alexa said. "I shouldn't have acted like that."

"Alexa, I haven't been able to stop thinking about you all day. I'm grateful you are bold because I have never been in this kind of situation before." His hands moved from her hair and traced down the sides of her arms. "But we better leave. I'm sure the men will be coming back soon."

His hand stopped on her fingers, then gently intertwined with hers. She squeezed her eyes closed, trying to get the mixed emotions inside her to leave. She needed to stop these feelings for him, because it was only going to get harder once she turned him in to the law.

"Then where shall we go?" Her voice trembled.

"I will walk you back to the main house. I brought you some stew. It's in your room." Ash pulled on her hand as they walked to the door.

"You were in my room?" A different kind of panic rushed through her. She had written on a notepad those items she had recognized at the ranch that belonged to her father, and the paper was on the table in the room. What were the odds that he hadn't noticed it?

"I knocked and you didn't answer. I thought you were ill." He laughed. "I suppose you fooled me." He opened the door and led them outside. "I left the stew on the table."

Would Ash be the type of guy that would snoop through a woman's things? From what she had known about him so far, he acted very respectfully, so there would be no way he would read what she wrote on that page. Would he?

There was only one thing she could do. Watch him for signs of mistrust. That would tell her if he read the list or not.

"That was so kind of you," Alexa replied.

After they were far enough from the men's sleeping quarters, she felt more at ease. But until she knew for certain if he read the list, she would continue to have her guard up.

"While you were resting earlier today," he began, "I rode to Granger's Pass."

She gasped and looked his way. "You did? Why did you do that?"

"I wanted to see if it was clear or not." He sighed heavily. "Sadly, it's not. There had been an avalanche and it hasn't been cleared yet. I suppose we could go around it if you wanted, but that would take much longer since we would have to create our own trails."

Slowly, she released a pent-up breath. "Then I suppose we will have to wait."

When they stopped in front of the main house, he released her hand. Thankfully, her heart stopped thumping so loudly. And because he hadn't brought up her list, she hoped he hadn't read it.

"Alexa, I must tell you that Mrs. O'Leary says you need to help around the house if you need to stay here longer. I let her know that we would find things for you to do around the ranch." He paused. "I hope that is all right."

Now she understood why Agent Montgomery had mentioned that Mr. and Mrs. O'Leary didn't often take in people who were just passing by. "Oh, Ash. I didn't get you into trouble, did I?"

"Of course not. As long as Mrs. O'Leary thinks you are working for her hospitality, then she won't bother you. Tomorrow, I'll be breaking in the steed we brought home today from Erie. Since you are such a skilled horsewoman, I thought you could help me."

Alexa nodded, thankful that he thought of her for doing something like that. "I'd love to help you." This would also be the perfect thing to do while searching for other stolen items. "I'm very grateful that she's letting me stay. I don't know how to thank her enough."

Now Alexa wondered if Mrs. O'Leary worked alongside her husband and Ash to pull off the robberies. Or was the woman's husband lying to her as well. Alexa was eager to find out.

Suddenly a scream of frustration echoed from inside the house, sounding like Mrs. O'Leary. Alexa ran beside Ash as they hurried inside to see what was happening.

"Where is it? Where did it go?" Mrs. O'Leary yelled. "Did you take it?" She pointed her fingers at some of the ranch hands. Then her gaze shot onto Alexa. "Or was it you?"

"What are you talking about?" Alexa didn't like being accused of something when she didn't know what was going on.

"My carousel. It's gone. It was there this morning, but now…" The woman's eyes narrowed, and her lips thinned as she pointed at Alexa. "I think you took it."

Alexa gasped, feeling highly insulted. "Why would you think such a thing? I would have never done that, especially after you helped me so much. Besides, I was in town all morning. But I also noticed it was missing earlier this evening. I figured you took it down to dust it off."

Mrs. O'Leary folded her arms, keeping the scowl in her expression. "That carousel was a gift. It was very expensive." Her gaze moved around the room, stopping on Ash. "I want every room searched, starting with the guest room where Miss Alexa is sleeping."

Alexa's insides trembled. Even though she didn't take it, she now worried that Ash had planted it in her room to set her up. After all, he went to her room, and he must have read the list. With her snooping through his room, that would have given him the chance to plant the carousel.

If the O'Leary's kicked her out, or told the sheriff she stole from them, that would make it extremely difficult for her to have Ash arrested.

Alexa followed Mrs. O'Leary up the stairs with Ash leading the way. The whole time, Alexa said a silent prayer. She wasn't done here. She didn't have the carousel… Ash did.

* * * *

Ash didn't like the way Alexa was acting tonight. She was hiding something, he just knew it. He thought that pulling her into his arms and kissing her passionately would wipe away the doubt that had filled him since he read the list she'd written.

When he kissed her, at first, the kiss seemed reluctant, but it had turned passionate very quickly. Then as if someone blew out a candle, she grew cold and pulled away, as if she had second thoughts.

He might not be the most educated person at the ranch, but catching Alexa in his room and the way she tried to convince him of why she was there, was like icing on the cake. Indeed, this woman should be in the theatre because her performance was spectacular, right down to the passionate kiss. After the kiss had ended, she seemed very distant. She was hiding something, and he wasn't going to stop pursuing her until he discovered what it was.

The porcelain carousel was an item listed on her notepad. There was even a checkmark next to it. He couldn't help but wonder if she was a thief, telling lies about being separated from her family just to get into a wealthy family's home to steal items to sell. That checkmark could be only one thing, she already took it.

Mrs. O'Leary marched up the stairs behind him while Alexa followed. Adrenaline rushed into his veins. Part of him wanted the older woman to find the item somewhere in Alexa's room, just to expose her lies. Then again, Alexa didn't seem to be that kind of person. She was sweet, incredibly smart, and very beautiful. No matter what this woman had done, he knew for sure that she had stolen his heart, and for that reason, he hoped she didn't take the carousel.

When they reached the top of the stairs, Mr. O'Leary moved out of one of the rooms. When the man saw his angry wife, his bushy eyebrows lifted.

"What on earth is going on?" he grumbled.

"My carousel is missing," Mrs. O'Leary snapped. "We are checking Miss Moore's room first." Her hand dropped onto the doorknob and twisted. Once inside, she grabbed the lantern on the wall, and lit it.

"If you took that item, you will find yourself another place to sleep tonight," Mr. O'Leary threatened Alexa. "I'm sure there is a spot in a jail cell for you."

"I'm telling you, I don't have it." Alexa hurried into the room. She moved over to the table and slipped her hand over her notepad, trying to hide it. The O'Leary's weren't paying attention, but Ash had.

The drawers were pulled open and what little items of clothing Alexa brought with her were pushed about. A rope was wound up and stuck in the second drawer. Mrs. O'Leary got on her knees and looked under the bed while Mr. O'Leary rummaged through the empty closet.

Ash noticed Alexa tuck the notepad in her skirt pocket. Her gaze followed the O'Leary's everywhere. When both stood, Alexa folded her arms and glared at them.

"Can I assume you didn't find it?" Alexa asked.

Mrs. O'Leary gave a sharp nod.

"You shouldn't accuse people unless you know for certain they took it," Alexa said. "I told you I didn't have it."

Mr. O'Leary moved out of the room first with his wife following behind him. She didn't even apologize for wrongfully accusing Alexa. If Ash didn't need this job so badly, he would leave, too.

Relief swept over Ash, knowing Alexa didn't steal the carousel. Maybe she wasn't planning on stealing anything. But what possible reasons would she have for logging certain items on her notepad?

Besides working with the steed tomorrow, he also needed to keep an eye on Alexa. He just hoped she stuck around long enough for him to find out what that list was about. He also received the impression that she was the type of woman who would eventually need protecting. Whatever she was planning couldn't be good.

TEN

The sun shone down onto the snow, almost blinding Alexa as she shook the rug against the railing. Never in her wildest dreams did she picture herself cleaning a home for someone who had just accused her of stealing. Thankfully, she came up with a good excuse to tell Ash as to why she had to stay. Being without her so-called family, she wouldn't have the funds to stay at the hotel in town until Granger Pass was cleared.

She actually didn't mind doing housework. She had dreamed of living in a home of her own someday, with a handsome husband who enjoyed taking the children outside and teaching them how to ride a horse. Their home would be in Colorado somewhere. Colorado was beautiful in the late spring and summertime.

If she became a Pinkerton agent, her wishes of a family would have to be put on hold. She chuckled softly to herself. Even though she had been married for a short period of time, she still felt like a spinster. Men only flirted with her now when she wasn't wearing men's trousers, which of course, didn't happen often.

Today was one of those days. Since her brown skirt was hanging to dry after the wash this morning, she chose to wear her dark red flannel shirt and denim trousers. Alexa felt so comfortable in them. At this point, she didn't care that the ranch hands were whispering about how unladylike she looked.

It didn't matter. She wasn't here to impress anyone. She was here to gather enough evidence to hand Ash Hawk over to the Pinkertons, and nothing more. Of course, she wished Agent Montgomery would get back to her about what they decided. True, they wanted her to work in the office, but she wouldn't take anything less than a field agent.

The high-pitched neigh of a horse drew her attention to the fenced area not too far from the ranch hand's sleeping quarters. Ash led the wild steed around the yard, trying to keep it from bucking. She focused on the handsome man's upper body. He wasn't wearing his duster since the sun was providing a nice spring warmth. His arms were rippled with muscles. Most likely that was due to the many years of him working in the mines.

Ash held the reins and circled the yard with the horse. Every so often he would stop and pet the animal's snout. He talked to the horse, but because she was further away, she couldn't hear what he was saying. But whatever it was, it seemed to calm the steed.

Alexa found it difficult to picture him as a bank robber. Yet the proof was there. He had her father's pocket watch, and he loved that picture, too. Even though she didn't see it, she was pretty sure he had that porcelain carousel stashed away underneath his bed.

She sighed and leaned up against the railing around the porch. Ash was one fine man. It was a shame he became a bank robber.

In a swift move, Ash mounted the steed and galloped recklessly around the yard. But it was another horse that pulled her attention toward the road leading to the house. She squinted, trying to see who the rider was. As he drew nearer, she gasped. What was Agent Montgomery doing here? Then again, she had told him where she was staying.

He stopped in front of the steps, dismounted, and then tipped his hat to her.

"Mrs. Moore." This time he didn't call her *Miss*, since he knew she had been married before. "I see the O'Learys have put you to work."

"Agent Montgomery." She cocked her head. "One must help out when relying on others."

"My thoughts exactly." He grinned.

Levi was a very handsome man. She should feel honored that he was paying attention to her.

"What are you doing out here?" she wondered aloud.

He walked closer, eyeing her up and down, even if his gaze lingered longer on her trousers. He grinned and nodded, leaning in closer.

"Is this what you look like when you're undercover?" He winked.

Chuckling, she rolled her eyes. "If you must know, my undercover *dress* is drying right now."

His attention left hers and moved around the ranch. She suspected he was taking inventory of everyone who was outside doing their chores.

"So, which one is it?" he asked.

"Which *one*, Agent Montgomery?" She shook her head. "I fear, I don't know what you mean."

"Which one is Hawk?"

She laughed, not wanting to give anything away. "What makes you think he's here? All I told you was that I was staying at the O'Leary's ranch."

Once again, Levi studied her face. "Of course," he said. "I'm just here to help you find your parents, that is all."

Feeling nervous, Alexa swept her gaze around them, hoping nobody was close enough to hear. She really wanted to tell someone about Hawk, and yet she didn't know who to trust. Perhaps she should give her trust to the Pinkerton man. After all, she was going to be an agent soon.

"You know," she whispered, "I'm not lost. My family is not missing."

"I have a secret to share, too." He leaned closer. "I know. I can tell a fake story when I hear one. That is why I'm a Pinkerton agent."

Alexa huffed, stepping away from him, folding her arm. That arrogant man. "Then what are you *really* doing here?"

His smile widened. "I'm checking up on you, of course. You seemed distraught yesterday for not being able to have lunch with me. I thought I would come and make it up and ask you to join me for lunch."

"You don't honestly think I believe you, do you?" Alexa laughed. "If you thought I was distraught, then you must not be a very good detective, because you didn't read me very well."

"All right, you got me. I knew that, too. You are a very bold woman. I want to help you take the bank robber down."

"I don't need help. I know what I'm doing. Remember, this isn't anything new for me. I have been doing this on my own for quite some time now," she reminded him.

"Tell me, Mrs. Moore, how long have you been capturing outlaws?"

"For a few years, since my husband died."

"And you consider yourself an expert?"

She rolled her eyes. "Of course not. But neither am I a novice." She sighed. Even though she had learned so much over the course of capturing thieves, she admitted—if just to herself—that trying to get Hawk to confess was getting harder every day, and she was running out of ideas. She also needed more evidence that tied the stolen items in the O'Leary home to Hawk.

"But now, let me ask you something, Agent Montgomery," she said before he had time to speak.

"You may ask me anything, Mrs. Moore." He smiled, making his eyes twinkle.

"What do you do when you feel you have found the outlaw, yet cannot connect that person with the crime?"

Levi arched an eyebrow as he ran the pad of his finger over his mustache. "That, my dear, is a great question. I'm sure all the Pinkerton agents have dealt with this a time or two. But what most of us have realized is that trusting our gut is the key. If we have doubts that something isn't adding up, then it is time to step back and analyze the evidence and the situation. First, and foremost, trust your gut, Mrs. Moore."

She flexed her hands by her sides. Did that mean Ash wasn't the thief she was after? Yet how could he not be when all reports gave his description? This was all so confusing.

"So," Levi continued, "do you need help finding the notorious Hawk?"

She chuckled and shook her head as she studied his handsome face. "Levi, why are you really here?" She folded her arms. "If I would have to speculate, I would say you came to observe my process in capturing a criminal… and you are hoping that I will give something away as to Hawk's whereabouts." The corners of his mouth twitched, and she grinned. "See, I'm good at what I do, too. That is why I should be a Pinkerton agent and not a wall decoration who works in an office."

From the corner of her eye, she spotted Ash briskly walking in her direction. She grumbled under her breath. Why did he have to interrupt her and the Pinkerton agent? Now she needed to act interested in Ash again… even though it really wasn't an act.

"Miss Moore," Ash announced, stopping beside her as his gaze bounced between her and Levi. "Is everything all right?"

"Ash." Alexa took a step away from Levi. "Agent Montgomery has come to tell me that he remembers seeing my family pass through town a few days ago." She shot a glance at Levi for him to hopefully chime in.

"Yes, they mentioned heading toward Colorado Springs." Levi nodded. "They also told me that their daughter had become separated from them and if I were to find her to tell her to meet them there."

"So, your family is found?" Ash asked without giving away his feelings. In fact, he wore a blank expression. It surprised her that his voice was full of disappointment.

"No, Ash," Alexa quickly added. "With that sudden snowstorm, I'm sure they are stranded somewhere." She placed her hand to her heart. "I pray they are safe."

"Don't worry, Mrs. Moore." Levi touched her arm. "Your father seemed to know what he was doing. There are many places to stop along the way to Colorado Springs. Rest assured, they will be safe."

The tender stroke of his hand made her uncomfortable, especially with Ash standing so near, so she moved onto the first porch step, but Ash pushed in between Alexa and Levi to separate them. From the hard look on Ash's face, she could tell he wasn't too happy with Levi being here.

"I think you don't know this woman as much as I do," Ash snapped. "She is not *Mrs.* Moore. She is *Miss* Moore."

Inwardly, Alexa groaned. Why had Levi made that mistake?

"Forgive me," Levi quickly rebutted. "I was certainly mistaken."

"You are forgiven." She smiled before turning to Ash and touching his shoulder. "I forgot to introduce you two. Ash, this is the Pinkerton agent I spoke with yesterday, Agent Montgomery."

Ash acknowledged Levi with a nod. "I'm heading inside for some water," he said. "It's nice to meet you." Ash stepped away and into the house.

Alexa sighed heavily. She could see that Ash was not pleased that she was conversing with another man. She knew jealousy when she saw it, and Ash was jealous. A small burn started in her heart, as if the flame had been lit again, stirring emotion into her body. She didn't understand why her emotions were clouding her judgment. She had most of the evidence that Ash was guilty, yet something just didn't feel right. She should never have kissed him.

"Oh," Levi's voice lifted. "I see clearly now. Too many roosters in the yard." He grinned again. "I should have guessed. However, I want you to know, *Miss* Moore, I'm here for you... to help you in any way you see fit."

"Thank you, Agent Montgomery. If I need more of your assistance, I will call upon you. Thank you for stopping by." She pulled on her flannel shirt, straightening it a little more.

Levi mounted his horse and took another look at her. "I won't be too far away." He shook his reins and the horse turned and they departed.

Alexa leaned up against the railing again. What just happened? Levi just took that trust that she had built up with

Ash and tossed it in the mud. Now Ash would think she had dove eyes for Levi. She needed to think of how to get that trust back.

* * * *

Ash scooped water with the ladle, dumping it in a cup for him to drink. Anger welled up inside of him. Why did God make him this way? Why did the Almighty allow Ash to be taken from his family and made to do bad things, and then never forgive him for doing them?

Because of his past life, there was no way he would ever find a woman who could love him. Ash's past would always haunt him. If God wouldn't forgive him, then why should Ash even try? Apparently, Alexa didn't want to be around him after he told her about working in the mines. Ash wished he had never shared that part of his life with her.

Alexa deserved a man better than someone like Ash. That Pinkerton agent was more suited for her anyway. Ash's heart ached, knowing that he lost her to that man. Ash could see the way she moved closer to Agent Montgomery as they talked. She had done that with Ash in the cabin the other day.

Something just wasn't right with Alexa. He could see it now. She was one of those women who searched for wealthy men to marry. That kind of lifestyle was something he would never be able to give her.

He slammed the cup down onto the table. There was no way he could trust her now. He must protect his heart.

He turned back to leave the kitchen and spied Alexa through the window. The men's trousers that she wore hugged her hips nicely, as if she were meant to be in them all along. Although she looked great in a dress, she looked more comfortable in rugged attire. He liked that.

There were many things about Alexa that he liked. He loved to hear her laugh and her eyes would twinkle as she spoke to him. Warmth filled his body as he thought of holding her in his arms and kissing her sweet lips. The woman confused him so.

The floor creaked behind him. Turning, he saw Mrs. Conrad pulling a gunnysack out of the cupboard. She carefully lifted it into her arms as if something precious was inside. The cook's gaze darted back and forth before she tiptoed toward the back door.

"Mrs. Conrad, do you need help with that?" Ash hurried toward her.

The woman stopped and met his gaze. Color drained from her face as her eyes widened.

"Oh, no, I'm good," she said quickly.

"That bundle appears too heavy for you to carry, so let me take it." Ash locked his hands around the package. Immediately, he could feel the outline of something that had a round base, and horse figurine. If he wasn't mistaken, this was the carousal Mrs. O'Leary had accused Alexa of stealing yesterday.

He narrowed his eyes on the cook as panic filled her expression. He wasn't sure how to confront the issue now. Why had she let Alexa take the blame?

"Please don't say anything," she pleaded in a whisper. "I need the money. The O'Leary's don't pay me well enough for all I do. Please, Ash."

"It's not right to take things that aren't yours." Ash knew that concept all too well. He was kidnapped from his family, which should never have happened, and he vowed never to live that kind of life again.

Her eyes turned wet with tears. "But I can't return it now. One of the pieces have broken off."

"I can fix it, but I'll put it in its rightful place on the shelf in the kitchen," he told her. "Just promise not to take anything again that isn't yours."

"I promise." She nodded and released the carousal into his hands. "Hurry before you are caught."

Ash knew exactly where to go to fix this. The barn had many tools and a workbench that Mr. O'Leary never used. Ash, on the other hand, used that workspace to repair things around the ranch. Besides being good at training horses, he enjoyed fixing things that were broken.

With the carousal hidden in the gunnysack, he hurried out the back door. He needed to make sure no one saw him. Especially Alexa.

ELEVEN

Torment filled Alexa to the point of helplessness. Why was this happening to her? Everything had been going just fine until Levi Montgomery showed up. She had Ash's trust, but now it was gone.

She beat the poor rug with a broom, taking out her frustrations on the only thing she could think of at the moment. Ash had been inside getting his drink for far too long. Did he sneak out the back way because a Pinkerton agent had been at the ranch? Yet she couldn't think that Ash knew she suspected him of being the bank robber. The only way for her heart to feel better was to try and talk to him, and the longer she waited, the more frustrated she became.

Alexa picked up the rug and returned it to the spot just inside the house. From the kitchen, she heard the chopping echoes as the cook prepared the midday meal. Alexa glanced in each room she passed to see if Ash was in there resting, but he wasn't there.

She stopped at the kitchen entrance and peered toward Mrs. Conrad holding a large knife as she aimed it over a potato. "Excuse me, but did Ash come through here?"

The cook's attention snapped up and landed on Alexa. Suddenly, the woman's face drained of color. Her hand trembled and she lowered the knife.

"What?" the cook's voice warbled.

"I'm looking for Ash. He came inside for a drink," Alexa repeated. "Did you see him?"

"No." Mrs. Conrad whacked the knife on the cutting board, slicing the potato. She scooped up the pieces and placed them in a pot.

Moonstone and Mistrust

Confusion filled Alexa. The cook was acting very strangely. "But not more than twenty minutes ago, Ash told me he was coming in for a drink."

Mrs. Conrad wiped her hands on her apron and looked toward the back door. "Oh, I suppose that was him who came in. I only heard the back door close."

"Thank you." Alexa hurried toward the back door.

As she stepped outside, her gaze wandered around the large yard. Ash wasn't anywhere she could see. She hadn't heard a horse leave the property when she was in the front of the house, so he didn't leave.

The large barn back by the horses' stalls would be the closest place for him to slip away and hide. She ran toward the barn to check.

Her mind spun with confused questions. What words could she say to him and gain his trust? One thing for certain, she needed to let Ash know that Levi meant nothing to her. She didn't love him like she did him...

Alexa stumbled, making her stop. *Love?* No. That was the wrong choice of words. *Cared.* Yes, she cared for Ash. She could never love a dishonest man who had broken the law.

Alexa picked up her pace again. She slipped through the wooden fence where Ash trained the horse. Her heart thumped louder as she neared the barn. Maybe if she just told him that he had nothing to worry about, then kissed him again, it would gain his trust in her. She swallowed hard. Kissing him always worked, even though it weakened her more.

Carefully, Alexa opened the door to the barn and moved inside. It surprised her how long and spacious the structure was, and there were so many horse stalls. A noise from the back corner led her footsteps toward the rear of the barn. Hopefully it was Ash and not Mr. O'Leary. That man made her very uncomfortable.

As she came near, she realized Ash was the person standing in front of the workbench. His broad shoulders and the black hair resting on his nape gave away his identity. Although she knew it was him, knots still formed in her stomach. They would be alone, thankfully. And she must kiss him to bring back his trust. But just thinking about doing the deed had excitement shooting through her. Would the ploy work? The wait was torturous.

"Ash?" Alexa called out.

He grabbed a gunnysack and placed it over whatever was in front of him, and quickly turned to face her. Guilt covered his expression. She caught him... but what exactly was he doing that he didn't want her to see?

"Alexa," he gasped. "I—I didn't hear you come in."

"Well, of course you didn't." She chuckled lightly, pointing to the entrance. "Considering the barn door is so far away."

He nodded. "This is a very large barn, but it's necessary for all the horses."

"I wondered that." She smiled, although her body quaked with anticipation. *Please, don't hate me.*

"I thought you were still talking to the Pinkerton agent."

"He left." She walked closer. "I came to talk to you. I could tell you weren't pleased with me speaking to Agent Montgomery."

"Stop." Ash pointed the narrow hand tool toward her. "I don't want you thinking I control you. That is the furthest thing from my mind. You can talk to whoever you want."

"I just met Agent Montgomery yesterday," Alexa explained. "He is very bold in his speech and a little too forward for my taste. He is not the man I want." She couldn't believe those were the words coming out of her mouth, but at this point, desperation washed over her.

Ash's expression softened. "Then if you don't want him, who do you want?"

"Ash Hawk." Alexa smiled. "I can't believe you had to ask that question." She moved until she stood right in front of him. "You are the one who makes my heart leap when I see you, and the one who is on my mind all the time."

His expression turned tender, and his gaze roamed slowly over her face, but resting on her mouth. She became breathless, and the urge to launch into his arms overwhelmed her. She must resist the temptation until the right moment, or her experiment wouldn't work.

"I'm not worthy of you, Alexa," Ash replied. "I can see the disappointment in your eyes when we talk about my past. I cannot change what I have done, even if I want to."

She placed a trembling hand against his cheek. She watched as his eyes turned the emerald color that she loved to see. He was enjoying her touch, she could tell.

"Ash, God loves you and He knows it wasn't your choice in what took place at the mines. You do believe in God, right?"

Ash placed the tool back onto the workbench behind him. He reached out and brushed a hand over her hair and twisted his fingers through it. An exciting chill ran down her neck. Why was it when they were together, she couldn't see him as the criminal?

"I have lost faith," he said sadly. "God never heard my prayers in the mine, even though I prayed nearly every day."

Pain tore through her chest. She stepped closer. "But Ash, God did hear your prayers and answered them. You and the others were rescued, and you made it out alive." A tear gathered in her eye, and she blinked it away.

His attention moved to her mouth again as silence filled the air between them. The beat of her heart quickened. This was the moment. If he didn't make the first move, she would.

Cotton dryness filled her mouth, and she licked her lips. Slowly, his head moved closer. Why was he taking his time? Her breathing quickened and she touched his chest, hoping he would speed things up.

She felt his hot breath breeze across her face, and she closed her eyes in preparation for the kiss. But after a few very long and agonizing seconds with nothing happening, she peeked under her lashes.

Suddenly, he shook his head and straightened. "This cannot happen. I struggle each day to get through life knowing everyone looks down upon what I've done. Alexa, you deserve much more than what I can give. And at times, I see the disappointment in your eyes when you look at me. It breaks my heart to see that on your face." He withdrew from her touch and turned back to the tool bench. He pulled the sack around whatever it was he was working on and lifted it into his arms. "I think the Pinkerton agent would be better suited to find your parents. Perhaps you should leave the ranch and stay at a hotel in town until Granger Pass is cleared."

Panic filled her and became suffocating. "No, Ash, I can't leave." This wasn't going how she wanted it to. She should have kissed him already. Now she doubted he would let her kiss him even if she tried. "I don't have enough money to stay at a hotel. I was lucky to run into you the other day. You saved me from becoming caught in the storm. Ash, *you* were the answer to my prayer when I asked God to help me."

His frown deepened as he turned and stepped away from her. She tried grabbing his arm to stop him but missed and her hand landed on the covering of the bulky object he held against his chest. The gunnysack slipped off, revealing what he had tried to hide.

A gasp sprang from her throat. *The porcelain carousel!* Surprise washed over her. She realized she had been correct in assuming he was the thief. Why else would he have it and try to hide it from her?

Ash yanked his arm away from her and picked up the sack from the ground. He scowled at her. "Please, just leave."

He jerked away as if she was covered with hot coals. His fast steps carried him toward the barn door's entrance. Panic surged through her, but it was different this time. Ash was actually running from her, even though it was only a brisk walk.

"Oh, no, you don't," she grumbled. "Not on my watch!"

There was no need to wait for proof of his stealing, yet he carried it with him. She must stop him now before the evidence disappeared again.

She gazed around the area, especially at the items closest to her. She needed something to help her stop him. Hanging on the barn's wall next to the nearest stall was her weapon of choice—rope.

Excitement pumped through her as she yanked it off the wall. Some people were gunslingers, a few were skilled at throwing knives, but not her. While growing up, she practiced lassoing the cows her family raised. She prided herself on being the fastest in the west.

Her hands moved swiftly as she tied a loose overhand knot in the rope. The rope was already coiled, so that saved time. She swung the rope high above her head, gaining momentum. Just as a bird takes flight, she released the rope and it sailed through the air, dropping perfectly around Ash and sliding down his arms. She gave the rope a hard yank, and it tightened around him, dropping him to his knees.

Alexa ran toward him, holding tightly to the rope so he couldn't get away. She stopped beside him and planted her foot in the middle of Ash's back, pressing him closer to the ground. Thankfully, he had dropped the carousel at some time during the struggle, so it would soon be hers for the taking.

As quickly as Mrs. Conrad could flip a pancake, Alexa had his feet bound and was working on his wrists. He rolled onto his side, wearing a shocked expression when he looked at her. Apparently, he was speechless as his gaze bounced between her eyes and the rope.

It didn't take long before his face grew red. She didn't have to be a genius to know the color was *not* from embarrassment. Any man would be highly insulted to have a mere woman hogtie them.

"What in heaven's name are you doing?" Ash snapped as he continued wiggling.

She tightened the rope harder, making sure he could not escape. He was much stronger than she first realized, but her hogtying skills could subdue even the wildest steed.

"You aren't getting away from me this time." Alexa tied the knot, feeling victorious.

He tried to separate his hands, but to no avail. "Alexa, you are hurting my wrists."

"Then stop moving, Hawk." Alexa gently knelt on his side and peered down at his face. "Even calves know when to stop fighting me, so I suggest you follow their example."

Ash relaxed, obeying her words. "Alexa, I haven't a clue what has come over you. Let me go, please."

She stood and walked around his body so he could see her better. Shaking her head, she sighed. "I'm tired of playing this cat and mouse game with you. I've been following your trail since Utah. Erie's bank will be the last one you ever rob, *Hawk*. If you tell me where the money is, maybe I'll sweet talk the sheriff into not tossing you into prison and throwing away the key."

His angry eyes narrowed, and his forehead creased. "What in the blazes are you talking about? Have you gone mad?"

"Stop lying to me, Ash. I know you are Hawk." She yanked on the rope still in her hand.

"Of course, I'm Hawk. That is my surname."

She shook her head. "No, you are the notorious bank robber, Hawk."

He gasped. "You have obviously mistaken me for someone else. I'm not a bank robber." Ash's glare darkened. "I told you I was kidnapped for years and held up in a mine in Utah. How in the world could I be a bank robber?"

Huffing, she folded her arms. "Your words are not going to sway me this time. I hate it when I'm lied to."

"*Lied to?*" Ash's laugh came out harsh. "Who is lying to whom?" He wiggled again. "You have deceived me from day one. Who are you anyway? The more I get to know you, the more I think you are not lost and looking for your parents."

Alexa paused as she thought about what he said. True, she had lied to him, but it had been necessary. Besides, she wasn't on trial here, he was.

"You aren't the one asking the questions, I am," she told Hawk.

He lifted his chin, stubbornly. "I'm not going to confess to anything until you tell me the truth first."

Inwardly, she boiled. But he was at least willing to trade confessions, so she might as well tell him. "You are the one living in a fantasy, not me. Look at all those people you have hurt. When you robbed my pa's bank in Santaquin, Utah, you put him out of business. You crippled my brother when you ran over him trying to get away. He will never be able to walk again." She moistened her dry throat with a hard gulp. "I was married, but once my husband died, I decided I wanted to become a Pinkerton agent. It has been my goal to track down—and capture—criminals in order to impress the Pinkerton Agency that I'm good enough to be one of them." She paused briefly. "My family is not missing. They live here in Colorado, and I can visit them anytime, but I've been quite busy since my father's bank was robbed, trying to find the criminal who ruined my family. I vowed you would pay."

Confusion deepened in his expression. "Alexa, you've got the wrong man. I would never do that."

"It is your turn now, Hawk. Tell me everything from the time you left the mines until now. And you had better not lie to me."

Ash sighed heavily, still frowning, and looking at her with mistrust in his eyes. "Alexa, untie me and I will tell you."

"Are you going to run? If you do, I'll wrap this rope around your neck so quickly that—"

"Alexa, I'm not running. In fact, I wasn't trying to run when you tied me up. All I was doing was taking the carousel back into the house. I needed to fix it, which was what I was doing when you came to find me."

Ash's voice was calm. In fact, he sounded defeated. She wasn't sure if he was lying or not just now. Was he running as she had thought, or was he just in a hurry to get back inside?

She really hoped she was right. Admitting she was wrong was a bitter pill to swallow.

TWELVE

After the ropes came off, Ash rubbed his wrists. It was a good thing he stopped struggling when he had. Otherwise, he would have rope burns on his body.

He hadn't taken his stare off Alexa since she hogtied him. Although she had removed his binds, she held a pitchfork. Having her think this way about him hurt more than he expected, and he didn't know if there was any more of his heart left to break. Who was this woman and why was she wrongfully accusing him?

"Start talking," she demanded. "I don't have all day."

"What do you want to know?" Still sitting on the ground, he leaned up against a bale of hay.

"I want the timeline of everything you have done since you left the mines."

He nodded. "Good, let's start out with an easy question." He sighed. "When Big Ed and her gang were arrested, all those in the mines were free to go. I made friends with a few of the men there. Benji, or Ben as we called him, and his little brother Al were my best friends. Their sister was the one who helped crack the case of the missing children and planned the mission to set us free. It was difficult to adjust to life after that, only because each of us needed to figure out what our skills were and try to find employment."

"Didn't you say your parents were dead?" she asked.

"Yes, as far as I know."

She tilted her head and narrowed her eyes. "What do you mean by that?"

"As I became one of the leaders in Big Ed's organization, I was forced to lie to the children to tell them their parents were dead or that their families moved away. I started to wonder if that was what Bowser did to me after he kidnapped me." Ash shrugged and shifted on the hard ground. "By the time we were discovered, I was a grown man and didn't need my parents. I stuck around Tooele County with Ben, Al, and Jeremiah, working odd jobs, whatever we could find. Jeremiah was another friend we made in the mines, but I needed more in order to make something of my life. Because I didn't know if Ash Hawk was my name, I wanted to find out who I really was, so I left and came to Colorado."

"But you robbed banks to get money," Alexa added to his story. "No one could travel without money."

Ash rolled his eyes. He wished she would believe him. "Do you want me to finish my story or not? Because it seems you have it all figured out. You think I'm guilty either way, so do you really want to hear me out or not?"

Alexa lowered the pitchfork and sat on another bale of hay across from him. "I'm sorry. You may continue."

It surprised him that she would want to do such a dangerous job and work toward becoming a Pinkerton agent. But he had to admit, she was good at pretending… and hogtying. He still couldn't believe that she had tricked him into thinking she was a helpless female who needed his assistance.

"We continued to work odd jobs like helping build wagons and rounding up cattle. Once we neared the border, Benji told me that he and Al were going to head back to Manti, Utah. Jeremiah and I continued into Colorado and went separate ways in Durango. I worked my way north until I found the O'Leary ranch. They needed more workers, so I got hired." He paused, if only to study her expression. For a moment, she looked guilty for judging him harshly, but then the stubbornness came back, and he felt disappointed again.

"I am not now—nor will I ever be—a bank robber, Alexa."

"Then tell me why I found several items that had been in my father's bank in certain areas inside the house." She nodded to the carousel sitting next to him. "The carousel is one that had been in my father's bank. It's worth a lot of money, you know."

"I can't tell you why the carousel was in O'Leary's home. The broken piece was brought to my attention, so I fixed it. But I didn't steal it from your father's bank. It was in this house when I arrived." Ash slowly stood, lifting the carousel, and placing it on top of the hay. "Alexa, I have been nothing but honest with you. However, you haven't been with me." He pointed to the item she thinks was stolen. "You can have it. I don't want it. I never did. I just wanted to fix it."

Slowly, the stubbornness disappeared from her beautiful face, and a look of helpless frustration replaced it. Ash didn't dare think she was finally believing him, but he hoped.

"If you aren't the bank robber, then who is?" she asked. "My informants told me the man's name was Hawk and that he had dark hair and green eyes."

He shrugged. "That isn't my problem. I'm innocent."

She stood up quickly. "What is in the carpetbag under your bed? What are you hiding in it?"

He shook his head. "You didn't hear a word I said, did you? I am not the bank robber."

"Just answer my question, please."

"Books." He folded his arms. "It took me years to learn how to read, and once I did, I found I loved a good novel. I have been gathering books along the way because I love reading so much. Now, if you don't mind, I have a job to do." He turned his back on her and walked away.

Thankfully, he made it outside the barn without getting roped again, so maybe she believed him. Ash was just so upset that she would even think him to be a bank robber. That was the most absurd thing he'd ever heard.

He could feel his heart ripping apart. Did Alexa mean anything that she said to him? It was hard to deny the growing feelings he had for her but giving his heart to her had been one of the worst mistakes he made.

Never again would he trust another woman.

* * * *

Alexa growled and pushed her horse faster. Tears stung her eyes, and all the blinking in the world wouldn't stop them this time. Apparently, not even the wind against her face could keep them at bay.

In the first time since she started looking for criminals, she had a sinking feeling that she had been wrong. She hadn't trusted her gut like Levi Montgomery told her to do. She had wanted to trust it, but instead, she let her mind believe that what she saw in the O'Leary house had been stolen by Ash.

She had been reading people's expressions for a while now, and Ash had been telling her the truth. He hadn't robbed her father's bank, and he certainly wasn't the one who crippled her brother.

A lump of emotion clogged her throat, and she swallowed hard. Her chest hurt so badly, she thought it would break. Did that mean her heart was shattered in the knowledge that she had lost Ash's trust and would never get it back? Or was she just hurt because she had been chasing the wrong criminal?

No. She had broken his heart, and in return, had damaged her own organ.

As she entered town, she slowed the animal. It was time to focus on where she was heading instead of the mistakes she had made. However, she needed to get past this. She needed to find the real bank robber masquerading as Hawk. If not, the Pinkertons would never accept her into their agency.

Right after her brother's accident, her friends and family had tried to talk her out of searching for the man named Hawk. They told her that she was too emotionally involved. Now she realized they were correct. In all the times she had captured an outlaw—or tried—not once did she feel like curling up into the fetal position and bawling her eyes out. Not once had she allowed herself to fall in love with her suspect.

Alexa needed help. She had to get out of this awful rut she was in. The only one who could help her was a Pinkerton agent. Only Levi would understand. She didn't dare let Dusty Sloan know how badly she had messed things up this time.

She stopped the horse in front of the Pinkerton building and dismounted. After tying the reins on the post, she wiped the moisture still gathered in her eyes. Taking a deep breath, she told herself this was the only way... the only way to make amends with Ash, and to get back on track with finding the right bank robber.

Admitting that she had been wrong would tweak her ego a little, but it must be done in order to move forward. She didn't want her heart to ache anymore. She wanted to breathe normally again, and to have Ash look at her with such admiration in his lovely eyes. Hopefully, that would happen again someday.

As she headed inside, she wrung her hands. What could she say to Levi? And would she like his answer?

Just before she reached the door, it opened, and Levi walked out. When he noticed her, he stopped short, and his eyes widened.

"Alexa? What are you doing here?"

"I... came to talk with you."

Levi gave her a helpless pout. "Oh, my dear Alexa, I cannot right now. I'm heading out on a case." He stepped closer, letting the door close behind him. He stroked his fingers across her cheek. "But I'm thrilled that you came to see me. Do you mind waiting? It will only take thirty minutes—no longer than an hour, I assure you."

What other choice did she have? Of course, she had to wait. The only other option would be to return to the ranch and see the hurt in Ash's eyes... If he looked at her, anyway.

"Yes, I'll wait." She gave him her best smile, which at the moment, wasn't that great.

"Splendid. I'll return momentarily."

Before she knew what was happening and could stop it, he leaned closer and kissed her cheek. Startled by his bold action, she inhaled sharply as her mind whirled with questions. He was already to his horse and mounting before her mind could think of a reaction. *Heavens!* What did he think he was doing? They were out in public, no less, and she was sure the town would be abuzz with gossip within the hour.

Then again, had she led him to believe she would accept such an outward display of affection? She must have or he wouldn't have kissed her. But it was too late to speak with him about that now.

She walked into the building and to one of the benches. Sitting and waiting wasn't her idea of enjoyment, and hopefully, the time would pass quickly.

Agent Sloan was at his desk with a middle-aged couple who looked vaguely familiar. She didn't know where she had seen them before, but she knew they had a sob story to tell Dusty Sloan, just by their forlorn expressions.

"But Agent Sloan, my wife and I feel that our boy is around these parts." The man twisted his hat on his lap as he and his wife sat on chairs in front of Dusty's desk. The woman dapped a handkerchief to the edges of her eyes as her lips trembled.

"Unfortunately, I haven't seen your son's description, Mr. Hawkins." Dusty reached across the desk and patted the man's arm. "Those who had been kidnapped to work in the Utah mines have all scattered. Who knows where they went."

By the mention of the word *mines*, Alexa perked up and her interest sharpened. She had researched this particular case so much when trying to find Hawk, she felt this incident meant more to her than most cases she had been involved with.

"I have heard," Mrs. Hawkins said in a squeaky, tearful voice, "that some of the children returned to the location in which they had been taken. If that is the case, our boy would be coming this way. Our land is only a few miles east of here. We live in Cottonwood County, and we haven't moved since he was kidnapped."

Dusty sighed and shook his head. Alexa could see the agent's frustration. Pinkerton agents always wanted to help, and it was disheartening when some things were just impossible.

"I'm sure my son hasn't changed that much," Mr. Hawkins added. "I'm sure his hair is still black, and his eyes are still green. I'm sure if you met him, you would think he was the kindest person in the world."

Bells went off in Alexa's ears as her head began spinning. For a moment, she thought she might lose consciousness. Yet why was she dizzy in the first place? Instead, she shook her head slowly, and tried to wrap her mind around the conversation she was eavesdropping on.

Black hair? Green eyes? Kindest man? If she wasn't mistaken, she would think the older couple were describing Ash. His last name was Hawk. Their last name was Hawkins. Ash had told her earlier today that the kidnapped children had been lied to and told their parents died, and they were given new last names.

She held her breath. Could that have happened to Ash? Was he really Ash Hawkins, this couple's long-lost son? What were the odds? And had her luck just changed from bad to hopeful?

If she was a Pinkerton agent now, she would want to unite this family that had been tragically torn apart, because that was what agents do—make people happy and find the outlaws who tore them apart in the first place.

Excitement sprang to life inside her once again. She must talk to these people to make certain that Ash is truly their son. After all, she didn't need to mess things up again, especially when it concerned Ash.

THIRTEEN

Alexa had been pacing outside for ten minutes already, waiting for Mr. and Mrs. Hawkins to walk out of the agency before Levi returned from his errand. She didn't want him knowing about her discovery—or what she hoped would be a breakthrough in Ash's life.

In her head, she went over how to begin the conversation with the middle-aged couple, and not to get them too hopeful. She didn't need to get them excited if Ash wasn't their son. That would be awful for them. She couldn't even imagine what they were going through right now.

When the front door opened, and the couple exited, Alexa stopped and waited for them to come closer. As soon as they made eye contact, she moved their way.

"Pardon me, but I saw you inside the Pinkerton office, and I thought to make introductions." She held out her right hand in greeting. "I'm Mrs. Alexa Moore, and I was inside and heard what you told Agent Sloan."

Both Mr. and Mrs. Hawkins shook her hand. "It's nice to meet you, ma'am," the middle-aged man said. "What can we help you with?"

"Well, I'm actually hoping to help you and your lovely wife." Alexa glanced at the woman who still dabbed her wet eyes.

"You want to find our missing son?" Mrs. Hawkins asked in a shaky voice.

"I want to try." Alexa nodded. "I know a little about the children who were kidnapped years ago to work in the Utah mines."

Mr. Hawkins nodded and frowned. "But our son isn't a child any longer. He is twenty-six years old now."

Alexa wasn't certain exactly how old Ash was, but she figured he was around that age. "Can you tell me more about him?"

"What do you want to know?" he asked.

There were so many questions she wanted to ask but didn't know which one to question first. "I heard you tell Agent Sloan that his eyes were green. What color of green?"

"Forest green." Mrs. Hawkins sighed. "He had the most amazing eyes as a child. People always commented about them."

Mr. Hawkins chuckled. "Even when our boy was happy, they darkened slightly. Sometimes we never knew if he was excited or angry."

So far, things aligned perfectly. "What kind of skills did your son have?"

Both expressions of the couple relaxed. Mrs. Hawkins even smiled.

"Our boy could do so much," the woman said. "He loved working in the barn with his father. They exercised horses every morning, and during the day, he helped repair the wagon wheels, or anything that needed fixing around the house."

Alexa's heartbeat skipped with encouragement. They were certainly describing Ash.

"Out of all his childhood friends," Mr. Hawkins said, "our boy was the one who told the truth. He had a difficult time lying."

Surprise washed over her, but the guilt she carried only became heavier. "That is certainly a rare trait in a child."

"That is what we thought, too," Mrs. Hawkins added. "But Pastor Williams said that our boy was a gift from God. He had the kindest heart. If anyone was hurt or sick, our boy was the one going to see what he could do to help."

Could Alexa feel anymore guilty? Why hadn't she listened to her heart when it told her he wasn't the bank robber? "Indeed, your son was extremely kind."

Mrs. Hawkins touched Alex's arm. "Do you think you can find him?"

Alexa nodded. "I shall certainly try."

"We heard," Mr. Hawkins said, "that those kidnapped children might return to the place that used to be home for them. We have lived in Cottonwood County since he was a small child."

"I'm sure your son will feel the need to come home, even if he isn't sure where home is any longer."

Tears welled up in the woman's eyes. "I pray you are correct."

"Where are you staying, in case I need to find you?" Alexa asked.

"Cottonwood County is a day's journey away. The snowstorm that hit the other day made us stranded in town. Until the pass is clear to travel, we will be staying at the Hamilton Inn." Mr. Hawkins pointed up the street. "Room Fourteen."

"Is there anything else that can help me identify you son?"

"He has a birthmark on the back of his neck," Mrs. Hawkins replied. "Even as a child, he wanted his hair slightly longer than the other boys to cover up the mark." She paused briefly. "Oh, and his name is Ashton Hawkins."

Butterflies danced wildly in Alexa's stomach. Indeed, Ash was their son. It was hard not to grin from ear to ear, but she needed to keep neutral in her facial responses.

"We just don't understand why he hasn't come home," Mr. Hawkins added. "We refuse to believe he is dead."

Alexa's memory opened to when Ash had told her about working in the mines. "I've heard that the survivors were brainwashed. The kidnappers probably told the children that they weren't wanted, or their parents had died. If your son is out there, he probably doesn't know you are alive."

Mrs. Hawkins placed her handkerchief over her mouth as a sob escaped her throat. "Oh, my poor boy."

"I will find your son," Alexa said with confidence. "I have a feeling he is not too far away."

Mrs. Hawkins grasped Alexa's hands and held them tightly. "I have prayed every night since he went missing that he would return to us. We will now pray for you."

Mr. Hawkins reached into his vest pocket and pulled out a tie-slider and handed it to Alexa. Immediately, she noticed the lovely design of a small black grizzly bear holding onto a rope. The bear's eyes were tiny white stones.

"I want you to keep this while you look for Ashton," Mr. Hawkins said. "If you see the man who was once our son, please show this to him to help him remember. This particular tie-slider was his grandfather's. It was something Ashton had always wanted from his Papaw."

Alexa nodded and ran the pad of her thumb over the white stones. "This is very beautiful. What is this gem?"

"They are moonstones." Mrs. Hawkins smiled. "Right from his grandfather's moonstone mine in the Beckwith Mountains. The mine is *Hawkins Gem*."

Mr. Hawkins placed his hand on his chest and inhaled deeply. "My grandfather passed away five years ago and left the mine to our family. If Ashton is still alive, his grandfather's mine is his inheritance."

Mrs. Hawkins touched Alexa's arm. "Please find our son."

She tried holding back her surprised expression. *Ash is an heir to a mine full of moonstone?* Knowing he had been forced to work in a mine, she wondered how he would react to this type of news. However, he would be more pleased to know his parents were alive.

"I'll keep in touch." Alexa nodded and placed the tie slider in her clutch.

She couldn't hide the bounce in her step as she hurried to her horse and mounted. She needed to ride like the wind back to the O'Leary's ranch to find Ash and tell him the wonderful news.

When she remembered that Ash didn't want to talk to her, a sharp pain in her chest replaced the excitement. He didn't trust her. If she told him about his parents, would he believe her at all? It was her own fault, and although she tried to convince herself she had been *undercover*, she shouldn't have lied. Yet telling him the truth wouldn't have gotten her very far.

Or would it?

Regardless of how he felt about her right now, she must try to reach Ash. He needed to know that his parents were alive and looking for him. Even if he didn't meet her gaze while she told him this good news, at least the truth would be out there. It would be up to him to meet his parents at the inn.

Alexa pulled on the reins, turning her horse toward the direction she needed to go through town, but she noticed a rider turning the corner and hurrying toward her. As he neared, she recognized Levi. His gaze locked on her as he approached her. Then she remembered that it was Levi she had come into town to see in the first place to ask about the horrible mistake she had made in assuming Ash was her criminal.

"Whoa!" Levi called out, bringing his horse to a stop. "Mrs. Moore, are you leaving so soon?"

"I... well, I suppose I have a few minutes." Alexa hoped he didn't want to kiss her again. She would let him know that her heart belonged to another man.

"Do you want to go back to the office or over to the diner?" he asked.

Knowing that she didn't want Dusty Sloan listening in on their conversation, the diner was the better place. People were in there, so it kept them in a public place in case he tried to make advances again.

"The diner is fine." She turned her horse back around and trotted toward the diner, which wasn't too far away.

Levi rode faster, arriving before she did. He was off his horse in no time, waiting for her to stop. He raised his arms up, grasping her waist to help her dismount. She didn't need his assistance but welcomed it anyway.

"You were gone longer than I had anticipated," Alexa said. "I figured I would just meet up with you later."

"Dusty sent me to the Sampson's Livery at the other end of town. Joseph was one of the bank clerks in Erie." Levi opened the door for her to the diner. "If you share what you know, I'll share what I know." His eyebrows lifted up and down a few times as he grinned.

Alexa stepped inside. The afternoon lunch rush was finished, and the place was mostly empty, save a few older gentlemen sitting in a far corner playing checkers and drinking coffee. Levi motioned to a table near the front window. She followed and allowed him to pull her chair out for her to sit.

"Why don't you go first," Alexa suggested. "I'm sure you have better information than I do."

"Oh, no, ladies first."

She doubted she would be able to change his mind now, but she still didn't feel right about telling him about Ash Hawk. She leaned her elbows on the edge of the table and leaned forward, staring into his lovely blue eyes. "Well, my lead sort of flopped. Please don't tell Dusty."

"Flopped? Pinkerton agents don't flop. Oh wait, you aren't one yet." He patted her hands. "Agents in training usually mess up. It's how we learn not to make that mistake again. So tell me, what did you do?"

"I accused the wrong man." She bowed her head. "But I know I'm getting closer, though."

The waitress came over to the table and placed glasses of water in front of them. "Are you ready to order?"

Alexa was too excited to be hungry, but she really hadn't eaten that much today due to the stress she was under. Ordering something light would be best. Before she could say anything, Levi pointed to the sign on the wall.

"We will have two cups of turkey noodle soup." He looked at her. "Is that all right?"

"Yes, I was about to say that."

Levi waited for the waitress to walk away before he grinned and gently squeezed her hand. "I'm happy to see we share the same taste in food."

Inwardly, she groaned. He had feelings for her, and she would have to let him down easily. This had never happened to her before, and she prayed the right words would come and that she wouldn't hurt him too much.

"I spoke to Joseph Sampson," Levi continued. "He said that there were two men who robbed the bank in Erie. Both men wore masks. Joe thinks one of the men was older because of the wrinkled, leathery look of his hands. But the second man," Levi lowered his voice, "has green eyes."

"It's the same bank robber that robbed my father's bank, then," she said in almost a whisper.

Confusion swam in her head. All the reports she had received described the robber as having green eyes. Yet it wasn't Ash. Had she met another man with such memorable eyes?

"It's Hawk." Levi kept his voice low. "There was another witness that came with Joe, his name was Calvin. He said he heard the older man call the younger one Hawk as they left the bank."

Alexa's stomach churned. Someone was making Ash look bad. Whoever the real bank robber was must be someone who wanted to ruin Ash's name and send him to jail. She must do anything to stop that from happening. Poor Ash's name was already ruined by this unknown bandit. However, once he finds out his real last name is Hawkins, then the old memory of Hawk could just disappear.

She tried to swallow the tightness in her throat. "Thankfully there aren't many men who have green eyes. We should round the all up and interrogate them until they confess."

"Easier said than done." Levi nodded. "Calvin also said he heard the younger guy, Hawk, call the older man O'Leary as they hurried out." Levi's face turned hard. "I've never liked Mr. O'Leary. As much as I want you out of that home, I think if you want to prove yourself a useful *future* agent, maybe you could spy on him, since you are already in the home."

The waitress brought the two bowls of soup and set them on the table before walking away. Alexa started eating as her mind filled with ideas. Levi was giving her this chance to prove to him—and probably to Dusty Sloan—how good she was. She must not let them down. But she still didn't know about telling Levi that she had found some of the stolen items from her father's bank. If she shared that bit of information with Levi, she was certain that he would come rushing in with the cavalry and she wouldn't have time to tell Ash that his parents were alive and looking for him.

She swallowed the food in her mouth. "Come to think about it, Mr. O'Leary seems to be absent from the ranch quite a bit lately. In fact, yesterday he and Ash, the man I was talking to earlier today, left for Erie that morning. They claimed to be picking up a steed, which Ash brought back. However, O'Leary didn't return with Ash."

Levi frowned. "I hate to admit this, but I think O'Leary is indeed involved. Alexa, if you find me some evidence of the robbery, I'll arrest him. I'm sure he won't go down alone. He will bring Hawk with him."

Excitement danced again in her stomach. Levi gave her a real Pinkerton assignment. Even though she already had the evidence, she wanted to find more. Where was O'Leary hiding the money he had stolen from Erie, and who was the man pretending to be Hawk? Alexa couldn't wait to find out.

FOURTEEN

Every time Ash looked up from his duties in the yard, Alexa was there, watching him. Seeing her pretty face and having her look at him with sadness in her eyes was such a torture. That woman had shattered his heart and seeing her everywhere was becoming too much to handle. When she had taken off this morning, he was pretty sure she was leaving, never to return. He had been so wrong in his assumption.

However, when she came back to the ranch, he noticed something a little different about her. It seemed she held her head higher. Had she thought she was right again? Did she assume she had found more evidence about his so-called guilt? Then again, her gaze wasn't smug. The twinkle in her eyes was almost as if she were elated about something.

He must stop looking at her, but it was difficult not to want a glimpse of the prettiest woman he had ever seen and remember the greatest kiss he had ever shared with a woman. But he wasn't the only one looking. The back of his neck tingled quite a bit, and he felt that she was watching him as well.

Ash must insist that she leave. Her bank robber wasn't at the ranch, and since she hadn't lost her family, she couldn't stay here any longer. Yet it bothered him knowing someone was tossing around his name as the criminal. It made him wonder if one of Big Ed's men got away and was out to ruin him. Not all the men who were in the mines led a simple life now as they tried to do what was right.

He carefully took the saddle off the O'Leary's new steed and hung it over the fence. He picked up a brush and slid it over the animal's coat, smoothing it. The horse neighed and nervously bucked.

"Do you talk to the horse?" The sweet voice of Alexa pulled Ash out of his thoughts. He was so focused on the animal, he didn't notice how close she had come.

"Yes. I make certain to tell the horse the truth, too," Ash snapped. It was hard not to feel bitter about this morning's confrontation.

"Ash, you must believe how sorry I am for thinking you were the criminal."

"I still think you should stay in town from now on," he answered.

"I don't want to. I want to be near you. I want to help you." She lifted herself onto the bottom board of the wooden fence and leaned against the upper board. "Ash, I want you to understand my point of view. Please, can we talk?"

A memory opened from when he was in the mines, listening in on conversations between Bowser and some of the older men there. It was mentioned that when a woman says *can we talk*, it usually meant the relationship was over.

Ash exhaled slowly. How could it be over when it didn't even have a good chance of starting? Her doubt and accusations wouldn't allow their relationship to progress.

"I'm not sure what more to say." Ash shrugged. "I have told you nothing but the truth the whole time, but it was *you* who couldn't tell the truth."

"Ash, I have been working undercover. As I mentioned earlier, I want to be a Pinkerton agent and when banks were being robbed, I knew I must find the responsible party. You see, back in Utah, my pa's bank was the first bank robbed. The man cleaned out the store. All the items my father had on display were taken, along with the money. The afternoon of the robbery, I was with Ma when it happened. But Gerald, my brother, was helping Pa at the bank. Gerald was returning from taking some trash out when a masked man came out of the bank. After securing the stolen items to his horse, he mounted and purposefully ran over my brother just because he was in the way." Alexa lowered her head. "My brother is in a wheelchair and will be for the rest of his life. I won't stop until I find the man who did this."

"And you picked any man with dark hair and green eyes?" Ash asked.

"After a few more banks were robbed, the word spread that people called him Hawk." She sighed heavily. "So yes, I was looking for anyone with dark hair and green eyes. After meeting you and getting to know you, I prayed you were not the man who did that to my family. When I saw you with the carousel that had been in my father's bank, I thought you were the robber." Her throat tightened with emotion. "I was dreadfully wrong, for which I'm so very sorry about. I was wrong, Ash, and I hope in time, you will forgive me."

He walked a bit closer. Her hair was braided and positioned over her shoulder. It was all he could do not to touch its silkiness. Touching and caressing wasn't a good thing to do.

Alexa's eyes filled with tears, and she blinked a few times while gazing at him. God help him, but he knew she was telling the truth. But how could he forget her mistrust and her lies? How could he forget that the first woman he had allowed himself to love was the one who had broken his heart?

"I still can't forgive you, Alexa. I don't enjoy being lied to. Even though I know you are telling me the truth right now, I can't help but wonder if you will ever do that to me again. You jump to conclusions too quickly, and I can't be with a woman who does that."

A tear slid down her cheek. "I was so very wrong about everything. It is difficult for me to admit that I messed up, but I did. I know it will be hard for you to forgive me, but I hope I can prove myself to you." She whipped one leg over the top board and sat. "I promise to tell you the truth, always."

"Well, that's a start, I suppose."

"Do you want to help me find out who is calling themselves Hawk?" Alexa asked. "I would love your help."

"I thought the Pinkerton agent was helping you." Ash could still feel jealousy running through his veins.

"He is, but he is doing it *his* way. I need to be undercover for my assignment. If I can figure this out, Agent Montgomery will put in a good word to Agent Sloan and I could be hired to be an agent, too."

Her smile was weak, and it didn't quite touch her eyes since the sparkle was missing. He tried not to feel as if seeing that in her eyes was what made him happy.

"I will help you, but only because I don't want to be mistaken for this bank robber ever again." Ash patted the brush in his hand. "What should we do now?"

She wiped away the moisture from her eyes. "First, I want to know a bit more about the mines."

He raised an eyebrow. Why in the world would she want to know that? That had nothing to do with the bank robber.

"Do you want to go for a walk?" he asked. "We can talk."

Alexa nodded vigorously and the enthusiasm in her expression returned, but not fully. He really did miss seeing her pretty eyes light up. She hopped off the fence and brushed off her skirt.

Nothing was said as she walked with him back to stable the horse. As they left the barn, he tried not to get too close to her. Even feeling her arm bump against him might make him change his mind about this whole thing.

"You said the men who kidnapped you brainwashed you, right?" Alexa asked, breaking the silence between them.

"Yes, I'm certain of it now. They had to do something to stop the children from crying all the time. Bowser was the man who constantly called me Hawk. I remember feeling uncomfortable at first when he called me that, and I don't know why. But he treated me like a friend, and I soon grew to trust him." Ash removed his hat and swiped the hair back on his head before replacing the hat. "Each child had a duty. Mine was to pick up the stones that were chipped away. I put them in buckets and hauled them to a cart on a track. As I grew a little older, I was the one chipping the stones from the wall while another child was picking up after me."

"Did Bowser tell you your parents were dead?" she asked.

"Yes. He said they had died in a house fire." He scratched his cheek, not really wanting to talk about his time in the mine, but if it was going to help catch the real person ruining his name, Ash would do it. "I recall hearing Bowser tell other children that their families moved far away because they thought *we* were dead."

"Did it ever occur to you that maybe they were lying?" Alexa kept her hands folded as they walked.

"I had no other choice but believe those who were my superiors. Perhaps that made me weak, but I was a child and wanted to make friends. I wanted a family, and at that time in my life, the boys and Big Ed's lead men were the only family I had. I wanted to believe them. In fact, I'm still that way now. When someone tells me something and they look sincere, I believe them." Ash's chest tightened. "That is why I'm still angry about this morning. Alexa, I trusted you until I found that list in your room. I didn't understand it, but what really bothered me was that you had written down the pocket watch that was given to me."

Sadness darkened her expression. "Those items were in Pa's bank. Your pocket watch was a family heirloom. When we were at the cabin and you took it out, that was when I really started to suspect you as the bank robber. I should have followed my gut feelings that told me you weren't the man I had been searching for." Her gaze dropped to the ground as her frown deepened. "You know that lovely painting in Mrs. O'Leary's sitting room? Well, that hung in my father's bank. And the carousel was in a cabinet on display for Pa's customers to see when they came inside." She shrugged. "I didn't know why you were hiding the stolen items in plain sight, unless you didn't think anyone from Utah would come to the O'Leary ranch in Colorado."

He stopped and looked at her. She halted beside him, meeting his gaze.

"Alexa, I didn't steal anything."

"I know." Her voice trembled slightly. "Although those items were from my father's bank, I don't know where the stolen money would have gone to."

"Is Mr. O'Leary a suspect?" Ash recalled thinking Mr. O'Leary had been acting a bit oddly when they went to Erie. "He was the one who gave me the pocket watch for doing a good job."

"Yes. I believe he has a lot to do with this." Alexa shifted from one foot to the other while wringing her hands. "Ash, I need to know... Do you truly believe your parents are dead?"

"I really have no idea. I'm not sure if I would even recognize them if I saw them on the street. All I remember of my childhood before I was kidnapped was that I lived somewhere in Colorado. I have a few faded memories of helping my father work in the barn and I loved to ride horses. But in my memories, I don't see the faces of my parents."

As he studied Alexa, he realized she seemed very fidgety. That wasn't like her at all. Something was bothering her, he could tell. Strange how he knew that much about her in the little time they had gotten to know each other.

He narrowed his eyes on her. "Alexa? Why do you keep asking me about my parents?"

Her gaze flew up and met his, and immediately, the sparkle had returned. She was certainly one fine looking woman.

"Oh, Ash." She grasped one of his hands. "I have been wanting to tell you, but I didn't know how."

He heard her swallow hard, and suddenly, the rhythm of his own heartbeat quickened. After all, she had been asking about his parents, which meant... No, it couldn't be what he suspected. How could he believe anything she said after what she had done to him?

* * * *

Alexa thought her heart was going to jump out of her chest. He watched her with his amazing eyes, which now appeared very leery. Did he know what she wanted to tell him?

She said a silent prayer that he would believe her, but especially, she needed God to help her word it correctly, so this wasn't something else she messed up. Ash deserved so much better, and she wanted to be the one woman to make him happy.

"What is going on, Alexa?"

Just as she thought. He was being cautious. But she couldn't blame him for that.

Breathing deeply, she tried calming her eagerness. She must make him believe.

"When I first came to town and visited the Pinkerton office, I overheard a conversation between one of the agents and a middle-aged couple who were there looking for their son who they suspected had been kidnapped to work in the mines. I didn't think anything of it, but then I saw them again this morning while in town." She stopped, trying to collect her thoughts that were jumping all over the place. "What caught my attention was when they said their son had green eyes and dark hair... and a very kind heart."

Ash's face tightened. He doubted her, she just knew it. She must keep talking.

"Forgive me, but my curiosity was piqued when I found the similarities between their lost son and the man I was falling in love with. I knew I had to ask more about their son to make sure he was the same person."

"Stop, Alexa." Ash shook his head. "I can't do this."

He turned and walked toward the field. She quickened her steps to keep up with him. Although he might not like it at first, she would *not* stop explaining.

"Ash, their last name is Hawkins."

His steps faltered, but only for a moment before he picked up his speed.

"And their son's first name is Ashton," she blurted out.

He stopped again and stared off in the distance.

"Ash, they told me how their son loved helping others because he had such a kind heart. Ashton's pastor called him a *gift from God*." She fished through the pocket of her Spencer jacket and pulled out the tie-slider Mr. Hawkins had given her. "The missing boy's father gave me this. He said it had belonged to Ashton's grandfather who owned a moonstone mine, *Hawkins Gem*." She stuck her hand in front of him, hoping he would see the tie-slider resting on her palm. "Mr. Hawkins said his son always loved seeing his grandfather wear this, and one day hoped he would have it."

He remained silent, but she knew he was looking at the heirloom. Slowly, he raised his hand and took, bringing it closer to study the object.

The thundering beat of her heart rang in her ears as she awaited his response. Even a reaction would suffice, but so far, all Ash could do was stare.

Seconds quickly turned into minutes. He didn't move, except for the several times he swallowed. Had he remembered about his parents and about his grandfather's tie-slider? Did he realize he was an heir to a very profitable moonstone mine?

What else could she say to make him believe her? Mr. Hawkins was sure by showing Ash the tie-slider, he would remember. Now, she wondered if Ash was this man's son. The only proof she had was his green eyes, dark hair, and kind heart. She prayed she hadn't made another mistake, yet her heart told her that the man she had fallen in love with was indeed Ashton Hawkins.

Finally, Ash's shoulders drooped, and he expelled a long sigh as if he had been holding his breath. His gaze swung toward her as he handed back the tie-slider.

"This isn't mine," he snapped and placed the item in her hand. He marched toward the field.

"Ash, wait!"

"Please, Alexa. I want to be alone."

Her heart sank, but she couldn't give up, and practically ran to catch him. "Talk to me, please. Why don't you think this is yours?"

He stopped so suddenly, she almost ran into him. His gaze pierced right through her.

"How can I believe a word you say?"

Alexa's breathing turned ragged as if she had run a mile. "Are you telling me you don't remember that tie-slider? You don't remember your *real* name?"

"I appreciate that you are trying to help me, but I'm not Ashton Hawkins."

She growled silently and bunched her hands into fists. He was so obstinate sometimes. "Ash Hawk? Seriously? How can you not see the connection, especially after knowing that the man, Bowser, lied to the other boys about their families?" She shook her head. "And as for not believing me, I begged your forgiveness. I'll do anything to earn your trust again. Ash, I care about you and want to see you happy, which is why I'm telling you about Mr. and Mrs. Hawkins."

"Those people don't want me."

Alexa's heart broke again. He folded his arms across his chest, appearing more wounded than angry. "I think they do, or they wouldn't have come searching for you."

"No, they don't. They want their sweet little boy who never lied, cheated, or did anything wrong in his life."

Ash's voice trembled slightly, and she thought she detected a tear, but he blinked rapidly, and she couldn't tell if he was feeling emotional right now. "I'm quite certain they realize what must have happened to their son in the mines, working for Big Ed. They read the newspaper articles when the story broke out. They aren't naïve. They just want to be a family again."

"Like I said," he snapped. "I'm not this person."

He turned to walk in a different direction, but she couldn't let this be the last of this conversation. She must instill inside him the need to fight his inner demons.

"Ash, before you walk away again, I have one more thing to say."

Thankfully, he didn't keep walking. At least she had that going for her.

"God is answering your prayers, even though you thought He never listened to you. He spared your life, and now He is giving back your parents. Please, trust God, and maybe, by doing that, you will find it in your heart to forgive me. And just maybe, you will start to love me again."

She didn't wait for his answer because she knew he wouldn't give her one. Instead, she made her way back to the ranch by herself.

FIFTEEN

Ashton Hawkins.

Ash groaned. He hadn't heard that name in so long, and he didn't know what made him bury it inside his memory. But although he was christened Ashton Hawkins, he was now Ash Hawk—the man who had lived a terrible life—one that his parents would never understand.

He rose from his bed and quietly dressed. The rest of the ranch hands were snoring loudly as they slumbered through the night. But sleep wasn't on Ash's agenda. He couldn't stop thinking about Alexa and those things she had said to him.

Did he believe in God enough to trust Him? It was difficult to ignore all the many blessings he had received once he had been freed from Big Ed's controlling hand. He had found wonderful friends along the way, and employment was always in his grasp—even though one of his friends hadn't had this kind of luck.

Then there was the day he had hoped a woman would come into his life, one he could love and trust and want to marry and have a family with. That was the day Alexa rode up to the ranch, begging for help. Of course, her story had been a lie. He believed her about *why* she led him to think she was someone else, but that didn't make the pain in his heart any less heavy.

He waited until he was outside the room before slipping on his boots. Being quiet was the only thing that would help him reach his goal tonight. Of course, he would need Alexa to do it, even if he didn't want to talk to her again. Yet she had the ability to clear his name and let the law know he wasn't a bank robber.

The house was quiet as he crept toward Alexa's room. He was relieved she hadn't taken his suggestion to stay at a hotel in town. At least she had better knowledge of what they needed to do in order to find the criminal who used his name.

One thing that he was thankful for while being in the mines for so long was the ability to see in the dark. Maybe that was why Bowser called him Hawk. Hawks had good eyesight, even though they weren't nocturnal animals, they could hunt their prey without problems in the daylight. Ash's eyesight was perfect in darkness as well as light.

Cautiously, he turned the handle on the door to Alexa's room. Once he stepped inside, he could hear her breathing deeply as she slumbered. He closed the door quietly and took slow steps over to her bed.

She was sleeping on her side, with one arm touching the pillow where her head rested. Alexa looked like an angel—what he imagined the heavenly creatures would be like, anyway. Two buttons of her nightdress had been undone at her neck, revealing a glimpse of her skin.

It was very improper of him to stand and gawk at her while she slept, but it was certainly enjoyable. He needed to wake the sleeping angel and not anger her for disrupting her slumber. He bent over and nudged her gently with his hand. She moaned and shifted her position, rolling onto her back.

Heavens, now he could see more of her neck. He must wake her before he became tempted by beauty because he knew how weak he felt around her.

Ash nudged her harder. This time her eyes fluttered open. He had his hand ready to cover her mouth in case she screamed.

"Alexa, don't scream." He placed his hand over her mouth, knowing she probably would. "It's me, Ash."

A small peep came out of her throat as she pushed herself to the sitting position, wrapping her hands over his to pry them off her face. Her eyes were wide with fear.

"Shh," Ash said. "Be quiet."

He waited for Alexa to give him a nod that all was well. She blinked several times before her body relaxed. She took his hand off her mouth.

"Ash," she whispered. "What are you doing here?" She pulled the blanket around her.

"Now is the best time to look around Mr. O'Leary's study. He and his wife won't be up for another few hours." Ash stepped away.

She flipped the blanket off and stood. He received a glimpse of her bare legs before the nightdress slid down and covered her limbs.

"It's so dark. We need a candlestick or something," she said.

"No. That would draw too much attention. Trust me, I can find our way through the darkened house." Ash grabbed her wrap lying over a chair in the room. He handed it to her. "What are we looking for?"

"More stolen items." Alexa quickly put on the wrap. "But mostly the money that was stolen from the bank in Erie. He must have a safe somewhere."

"He does." Ash's mind opened, letting him see exactly where it was located. "It's in his study."

She grabbed his hand. "Lead the way."

It felt good having her hand in his again. Memories from their time in the cabin returned in full force. He couldn't be certain, but it felt as though his cold heart was beginning to melt.

Ash led them down the stairs to the main hallway. To be sure everyone was asleep, he stopped, keeping her hand in his. He listened. Thankfully the house was still quiet.

Ash turned down the hallway leading to Mr. O'Leary's study. The door was closed, so he opened it—being as quiet as possible—and stepped inside.

"He has a hidden wall over here," Ash whispered. "I walked by the room one time when he didn't know I was here, and I saw him getting into the safe." Ash released Alexa's hand as he walked to the place on the wall covered by a large mirror.

"I'm going to look over here," Alexa replied. "My eyes are adjusting to the darkness now."

She walked to Mr. O'Leary's desk, waving her hands out in front of her to feel the way. He chuckled lightly. It was obvious that she still struggled to see, especially when she bumped into the desk and immediately put her hands on it to steady herself.

Ash carefully moved to the wall and removed the mirror. Sure enough, the safe was there, just as he suspected. He lifted the padlock and shook it, hoping it was unlocked. He glanced around the dark room. The time he had observed Mr. O'Leary in the safe, Ash also noticed that the man took the key to the far wall.

Frowning, Ash scratched his chin. Would his employer have hidden the key just as he hid the safe?

He glanced at the wall in question. Two paintings hung close together. Curiosity moved him to the first painting. He carefully took it down and looked behind it, but nothing was there. As soon as he removed the second painting, he heard something knocking against the wooden frame. It was the key!

He grabbed the key and swung toward Alexa. She was holding up a piece of paper toward the window. She turned the paper a few times and leaned in closer to it.

"Ash!" Excitement filled her voice. "Come here."

Ash moved behind her to see what she was looking at. Alexa handed the paper to him.

"It has the words *Friday night, Hawkins Gem*," she whispered. "That is the name of your family's moonstone mine."

Ash took the paper and observed it closer. Sure enough, it had those words. But why?

"Ash," she continued. "I think Mr. O'Leary and his accomplice are going to rob your family's mine. Moonstones are worth lots of money, I'm sure."

Anger stirred in Ash's veins. First the bank robber was trying to ruin his name, and now this person wanted to steal from his family. Ash suspected the mine was his family's only income. This needed to stop now.

"I think you should let your Pinkerton friend know about this. Tomorrow is Friday. We could stop them." Ash put the paper down.

"Yes, I believe you are correct. We'll tell Agent Montgomery in the morning." She paused. "Did you have any luck on the safe?"

"I found the key." He held it up in front of her face, just in case she still couldn't see well.

He moved to the safe and knelt in front of it. "If the money is in there, do we take the money out?"

"No, we just need to make sure it's there. If it is, then we let Agent Montgomery and Agent Sloan know. They will work with the sheriff and have it confiscated." Alexa crouched down next to him. "Open it."

Ash slid the key inside the padlock and twisted. The unlocking clank echoed in the quiet room. He pulled the padlock off and looked at Alexa. Her eyes were wide with excitement. He had to admit, she would make a really great Pinkerton agent.

"You do it," he whispered. "This is your find, not mine."

She placed her hand on the handle and pulled it open. Ash's jaw dropped as surprise washed over him. Alexa had been correct. The safe was full of money, so much more than a person should keep in their house.

She reached in and pulled out a bundle of papers. Bonds. The backs were stamped with the words *Erie, Colorado.*

"Ash, this is it!" Alexa leaned over and kissed him on the cheek. He didn't have time to stop her, but he was also caught up in the excitement. Her lips tingled on his cheek, which would leave an everlasting impression. Now he ached for more.

The floor creaked outside the room, from down the hallway. Panic filled him. They were going to be caught. Hopefully Mr. O'Leary didn't have his gun on him, otherwise they would be shot for sure.

"Hide." Ash pointed to the back closet. "Don't make a sound."

Alexa quickly stood, bumping into a few pieces of furniture as she made her way to the closet. Ash tossed the bonds back inside the safe. His hand touched a sack. Out of curiosity, he pulled it out. It was full of coins. How long had Mr. O'Leary been doing this? He had enough money to buy at least two more ranches—plus the horses.

"Don't move."

Ash stilled as his heart sank in his chest. Here he was doing the very thing people accused him of, yet he was innocent.

"Raise your hands where I can see them," the man said in a quiet voice.

Ash did as instructed, but he also peeked over his shoulder. A man wearing a trench coat, pointed a gun toward him. It was the Pinkerton agent that Alexa trusted. Of course, he wasn't sure if he should feel relieved or not.

"Be quiet or Mr. O'Leary will hear you," Ash whispered, as he stood. "I'm actually surprised he hasn't come in yet."

"I knew it was you," Agent Montgomery said with a growl as he stepped closer. "Caught you red-handed, too."

Ash looked down and the bag of coins was still in his hand. He sighed in desperation. "It's not what it looks like, you see—"

"You are Hawk, right?" Agent Montgomery took a few more steps closer. "Green eyes, dark hair? Yeah, I knew it was you when Mrs. Moore watched you earlier."

"I'm not the man you are after," Ash argued again. He was getting tired of this. "Look, we have proof." Ash reached over to the desk to retrieve that paper Alexa found.

"Don't move or I'll shoot. You know, I do have orders to bring you in dead or alive." Agent Montgomery snarled, making his mustache dance on his upper lip.

Ash's heartbeat quickened. "If you just talk to Alexa, she will explain everything."

"*Alexa?* You are on a first name basis with her now?"

"Levi, don't." Alexa stepped out of the closet. "Ash didn't do it."

Moonstone and Mistrust

"Alexa, just stay where you are. I've got this under control," Agent Montgomery warned.

"And so do I." She took another step closer. "He is not the man we are after."

Ash prayed the agent would believe her but as he watched the man's expression, doubts popped into his mind. Agent Montgomery certainly had feelings for Alexa and was finally coming to realize she didn't return his feelings.

Ash glanced at Alexa. The tenderness in her expression when she looked at *him* let him know which man the woman truly loved.

However, now was not the time to worry about that. The Pinkerton agent would be upset with this new realization, and with him still holding the gun, Ash couldn't see this ending well.

"Levi, put down the gun," Alexa said as her voice softened. "I will explain everything."

Agent Montgomery barked a harsh laugh, aiming a glare at Alexa. "You are in love with a criminal, aren't you?"

Ash worried that the agent was not going to understand at all. Using this slight distraction with Alexa, he reached again for the paper on the desk, hoping that would convince the man. Agent Montgomery whipped his gaze back to Ash. The man's arm tightened as he steadied the pistol toward Ash.

"Don't!" Alexa jumped in front of Ash, holding out her hands as she faced Agent Montgomery.

A spark flew from the barrel of the pistol. *Bang.*

"No!" Ash shouted.

Alexa stood in shock for a moment before she looked down at her shaking—and bleeding—left hand. Immediately, blood soaked her white nightdress, forming around the lower portion of her left shoulder and spreading quickly. Ash grabbed her, just as she fell against him. Her eyes locked with his and confusion covered her face.

She brought her left hand up to his face and caressed it. "You aren't the bank robber. Convince Levi…" She fell limp in his arms.

SIXTEEN

Helpless, Ash stared at the unconscious woman. Blood coated her chest quickly and dripped from her left hand to the floor. The gentle rise and fall from her bosom let him know she was still breathing, but for how long, he couldn't be certain.

He pierced the agent with a glare. "Grab an afghan or something. We need to get her to the hospital before she dies." His throat grew tighter. Alexa couldn't die on him. Not now. Not when he still had feelings for her.

"Let me take her." Agent Montgomery held out his arms.

"No. You've done enough already," he snapped. "Besides, you need to go after Mr. O'Leary." Ash lifted Alexa in his arms. "Look inside the safe. That is the money and bonds that O'Leary stole from the Erie bank."

The slamming of the house's back door alerted Ash to what was probably happening. "O'Leary is getting away. Go capture your true thief."

Ash didn't wait for Agent Montgomery to leave out the door first. Every second counted right now, or Alexa would die. He made it out of the house, just in time to see Mr. O'Leary fleeing on a horse.

Zach and Trevor Dalton were the first of the ranch hands to rush out of the sleeping quarters from the noise of the gunshot. They looked at Ash and immediately hurried toward the barn. By the time Ash arrived, a horse was hooked up to a wagon ready for him. The brothers assisted Ash with helping to climb in the back. He held her while Zach moved to the driver's seat.

Ash kept pressure on her shoulder and hand, hoping to stop the bleeding. Trevor sat beside him, assisting any way he could.

"Breathe, Alexa," Ash encouraged. He could feel her chest heaving against him, but she struggled with every breath. "Faster, Zach. Go faster."

Ash's eyes filled with liquid. It had been a while since he was this emotional. But in the past few days, between the good and bad, Alexa had grown on him. He was willing to give her a second chance since she seemed sincere. He could finally see she was trying to make amends.

It had been a very long time since he had prayed. If she died without knowing that he had forgiven her, well, he might as well die, too. He needed to express his feelings for her because he knew now that he loved her.

"Lord, I'm so sorry I gave up on you," Ash whispered as he closed his eyes. "You were blessing me, and I didn't see it. You sent me an angel to lead me back to my family, and I rejected her. Please forgive me, Lord. Please don't take my angel away from me. I need her so much..." His voice broke as a tear rushed down his cheek. He tightened his arms around her and kissed her forehead. "I love you, Alexa Moore."

After what seemed like an eternity, Zach stopped the wagon in front of the hospital. Carefully, Ash lifted her out of the wagon with Trevor's help. Zach rushed inside to find the doctor.

Her blood soaked through his shirt as well as stained his hands. He didn't care. If God would let him, he would switch places with her. Ash was the one who had led a terrible life and deserved to be punished, not her.

When he stepped inside the dimly lit hospital, he noticed the color was drained from Alexa's face. His heart cried out. No! She couldn't die. "Alexa, please come back to me."

A gurney was waiting for her, and he placed her on it.

"She was shot," Ash replied. "Please help her."

"We'll do our best." One doctor and two nurses rushed Alexa to the back of the building.

Ash's chest was so tight, it was hard to breathe.

Zach placed his hand on Ash's shoulder. "I've been here before, and there is a chapel nearby. Do you want to go?"

Ash nodded and dragged his feet as he walked with Zach. Lit candles brightened the peaceful room slightly. It was hard to feel peace when Alexa's life was hanging from a thread.

Five pews lined the small chapel. Near the front was a picture of Jesus. He recognized the painting from when he was a child going to church with his parents. Ash wished he had his parents here now to share in his grief. But would they understand what happened to him in the mines and how he had to lie to those children? Would they forgive him... and still love him? He wasn't their innocent—and naïve—boy any longer.

He collapsed in the first pew and stared at the painting of the Savior. Ash didn't need to feel alone anymore. He had someone. He had Jesus. Peace settled in his heart, creating a slow burn. He realized he had never been alone in the mines. The Lord had been with him the whole time.

Tears flowed down his cheeks, and he wiped them with his bloody hands. He knew God forgave him from the way he was brought up in the mines, with evil teaching him. He'd had no choice in that type of lifestyle. Now he did. Thankfully, the Light of Christ was always in him, and he knew right from wrong. Changing his ways as soon as possible was his redemption. God loved him.

* * * *

"Ash." A voice echoed in his ears. "Wake up." He felt his body move with someone pushing him.

He blinked open his eyes, hoping everything with Alexa had been a nightmare. Sunlight streamed through the stained-glass windows in the chapel. It wasn't a dream. He must have fallen asleep, and now it was morning. He quickly straightened, causing his head to swim with dizziness.

"Don't you lose conscious on me," the man standing next to him said.

Ash looked up to see Agent Montgomery standing next to him. His expression was etched with concern.

"What are you doing here?" Ash grumbled.

"I came to see about Alexa."

"Has the doctor said anything?" Ash asked.

"No," Agent Montgomery replied. "But you need to wash the blood from your face and hands. You look like you've been in a battle."

"What time is it?" He patted for his pocket watch, but it wasn't in his trousers.

"It's about nine-thirty," Agent Montgomery replied. "I got here as quickly as I could."

Ash glared at the agent, "Are you arresting me? Because I'm warning you, I won't go peacefully. I'm not leaving Alexa."

Agent Montgomery shook his head, frowning. "I'm not arresting you. I'm here to apologize for accusing you. I know you aren't the bank robber." He leaned back on the seat. "I went after Mr. O'Leary. I got him. He is behind bars now."

"There is still another person, someone who is using my name. I don't think O'Leary was calling himself Hawk," Ash said. "But I can't think right now. I need to find someone who can tell me what's going on with Alexa."

"One more thing," Agent Montgomery added, swallowing hard. "I feel terrible for what I've done. I pulled the trigger when I shouldn't have. I—I've never done that before." He put his head in his hands. "If she dies, I don't know what I'll do."

Ash stood and placed his hand on Agent Montgomery's shoulder. "I've known for a while how much you care for her. I want you to know, I love Alexa with all my heart. When I'm with her, she makes me a better person. But you can still pray for her. Please, do that for her."

Agent Montgomery nodded.

Ash walked out of the room, leaving the Pinkerton agent alone with God and his thoughts. Zach and Trevor were asleep on chairs just outside the chapel. They were good friends. Ash was lucky to have a few of them.

A nurse carrying some white linen rounded a corner. She glanced at him but continued down the hall.

"Excuse me, ma'am. Do you have any information about my friend?" he asked.

"We aren't sure yet," the nurse replied. "She lost a lot of blood."

His chest tightened, wishing he could give her some of his blood. "What can I do?"

"Just wait. Time will tell," she replied. "You should go wash up." The nurse pointed to the door that led outside. "There are toiletries out there."

Ash nodded and stepped outside to a water basin. A small mirror hung nearby. He glanced at his reflection. Streaks of blood and dirt marked his face. He looked at his hands and they were stained with Alexa's precious blood. It was hard not to sob like a baby. If he hadn't taken her to the study... No, he must not blame himself. The Pinkerton agent was at fault. Ash needed to be strong right now.

After vigorously scrubbing for a few minutes his face and hands were as clean as they could be without taking an actual bath. He stepped back inside the hospital and wandered around the waiting room. The front door opened and in walked a tall man with broad shoulders and an older couple followed behind him.

The tall man looked familiar. He was with the Pinkerton that Ash saw the other day when he returned from Erie. Because the tall man dressed similarly to Agent Montgomery, Ash suspected it was the other agent.

The man took large steps and stood in front of Ash. "I'm Pinkerton Agent Dusty Sloan," he greeted. "Have you any word yet on Mrs. Moore?"

It was difficult hearing other people speak of Alexa as *Mrs.* Yet she was.

Ash shook his head. "She lost a lot of blood. All they are telling me is to wait and time will tell. Agent Montgomery is in the chapel if you are looking for him."

Dusty Sloan nodded. "He is devastated about what happened, and frankly, so am I. Things like this don't usually happen. You see, someone is making you out to be the bank robber. We now know you aren't the man we are searching for." Agent Sloan looked over his shoulder toward the older couple behind him. "However, you might be the man *they* are looking for." He patted Ash's arm and stepped aside.

The older couple stared at him with wide eyes. The woman seemed very familiar. Tears welled in her eyes, and he could see that she was fighting the urge to run to him. A huge lump gathered in Ash's throat, making it hard to swallow. He knew these people, but they were older than he remembered.

"Ma? Pa?" Ash's voice cracked.

The couple rushed to him, throwing their arms around him and they sobbed. His mother showered him with kisses and his father had a hard time letting go of Ash. It surprised him how grateful he felt, knowing that they were finally reunited. Not every boy who had been kidnapped to work in the mines had this good fortune. This was the happiest and saddest day of his life.

"We heard that Mrs. Moore was shot," Pa said, wiping his tears from his face as he withdrew. "She was helping us find you."

"She protected me," he replied. "She took the bullet for me." He blinked back the tears trying to impair his vision. "Alexa can't die. I love her. She needs to hear me say that to her."

His father grasped his hands. "I knew there was something special about her when we met her. We will pray for her."

The three huddled in a corner and his pa recited a beautiful prayer on Alexa's behalf. Hearing his pa's voice brought back the memories that had been hidden. Ash remembered his pa teaching him how to ride a horse and take care of them. Going fishing in the nearby pond was one of his favorite things to do.

"When did Papaw die?" Ash asked.

"Five years ago," Pa replied. "He left us the mine. Do you remember Hawkins Gem?"

Today is Friday. Even though Mr. O'Leary was behind bars, there still was someone out there pretending to be Ash Hawk. He needed to stop them.

"Pa," Ash put his hand on his father's. "The mine is going to be robbed tonight. I don't know when, just sometime tonight. I don't know by who, either, but I will let Agent Sloan and Agent Montgomery know. Someone has been ruining my name, and I don't know why. I promise not to let them destroy Hawkins Gem."

After telling the Pinkerton agents about the note Alexa found on O'Leary's desk, Ash sat with his parents in the waiting room. He tried his hardest to pay attention to everything they told him about things that had happened in the past years. It was hard to stay focused when he knew Alexa wasn't out of danger yet. Zach had returned to the ranch and brought back another shirt for Ash to change into.

Just after lunch time, Ash stood and walked the halls again, looking for someone to give him any information about Alexa. A doctor exited one of the rooms, appearing exhausted. He wore a solemn expression as he walked.

"Doctor," Ash held up his hand for the man to stop. "Please, I need some information. My friend was brought in early this morning with a gunshot wound. We have been waiting all morning for an answer. I need to know what is going on."

The doctor's frown deepened, and he shook his head. "I'm sorry, sir. Your friend died ten minutes ago."

SEVENTEEN

Ash couldn't breathe. In fact, his heart may have stopped beating, then skipped a few times to start up again. He must have heard the doctor wrong. Alexa couldn't be dead.

"Wh—what?" Ash shook his head in disbelief.

"Your friend lost a lot of blood. There was nothing we could do. I'm very sorry."

Ash's legs trembled and he grabbed the desk to keep from falling. His vision blurred and tears leaked from his eyes. What was God doing to him? Ash poured his soul out to Him just hours before. Did the Lord not hear? Why take Alexa? Unless it was punishment for the things Ash had done.

"No... no," Ash sobbed, clutching his chest. "She can't be gone."

"Can I have the nurse get a priest for you?" the doctor asked.

An arm went around Ash, keeping him from falling over. He looked up to see Agent Montgomery holding him tightly. The man also had moisture in his eyes. Even though this was the man that was responsible for killing her, at this moment, the only person Ash could blame was himself. If Ash wouldn't have reached for the paper on the desk to show the agent, the man wouldn't have shot the gun.

Ash buried his head against Agent Montgomery's shoulder and sobbed.

"Doctor," a woman's voice echoed in Ash's ears. "The patient in room six is awake. She is delirious, I think. She keeps requesting ashes and a hawk. Do you want me to give her more medicine?"

Ash pushed away from Agent Montgomery and stared at the nurse. He wiped his face quickly. "My name is Ash. Ash Hawk."

The doctor stared blankly at Ash for a moment. "Oh, the young lady is your friend?" he chuckled lightly. "My mistake, forgive me. She is alive. Apparently, she blocked the bullet with her hand, shattering a few bones, but it slowed the momentum of the bullet and it ricocheted, landing in her upper left shoulder, barely missing her lung. Not sure how that happened."

"It is a miracle, if you ask me," the nurse replied. "They do happen, you know."

Relief flowed through Ash as more tears streamed down his face. Agent Montgomery patted Ash on the shoulder again.

"Go to her. Alexa loves you," he replied.

Ash smiled, although his lips trembled. He knew she loved him. She sacrificed her life for him, and thankfully, God saw fit to keep her alive to be with Ash. *Thank you, Lord.*

"Follow me, sir," the nurse said. "I'll take you to her."

Ash practically sprinted down the hallway, passing the nurse a few times. He knew how to count, and room six was not too far away. The nurse motioned to the room.

"She needs rest," the nurse said. "Don't be long."

Ash hurried past the nurse and entered. It was a small room, but still held two beds. Only one was occupied. Alexa's eyes were closed as she rested on the bed. Her left hand was thickly bandaged. Gauze wrapped around her chest and shoulder, but a blanket covered most of her body.

Her bosom rose and fell smoothly now. She was alive! God brought Ash's angel back to him.

He sat on the chair next to her bed and gently cupped her right hand against his. Ash leaned in and kissed her knuckles.

"Ash?" Alexa whispered.

"Yes, my angel." He kissed her knuckles again. "It's me."

"He didn't shoot you," she weakly said. "I was worried."

Ash shook his head. "But I would rather he had shot me. You didn't deserve this." He reached up and stroked the side of her cheek. "I'm so relived you are alive."

"That makes two of us." She shifted in the bed and groaned. "I'm not sure which hurts more, my hand or my shoulder."

"I know what hurts me the most. It is seeing you in pain. If God would let me, I would switch places with you."

"Oh, Ash," she smiled weakly. "God is blessing us both."

He smiled. "My parents are outside. They were worried about you, too."

"You found them. I'm so happy." She closed her eyes.

"Alexa, before you fall asleep, I want you to know something." Ash leaned in closer.

She opened her tired eyes and blinked a few times. "What? That I was foolish for stepping in front of the bullet?"

"Well, yes, but that isn't it. Alexa, I'm sorry for being hurtful to you when I discovered your lie. I understand now why you did it. Will you forgive me?"

"I already have." She moved her right hand to his lips, stroking him with her fingers. "Do you forgive me for lying?"

He kissed her fingertips, wishing it were her lips, instead. Ash nodded. "Of course... over and over again. And one more thing. Alexa, I love you."

She smiled as a tear slid down the side of her face. "I love you."

"Do you love me enough to marry me?"

Her smile widened. "Most definitely."

* * * *

"I'm coming with you." Ash folded his arms in protest as he glared at the two Pinkerton agents. "Unlike you two, I can see in the dark mines without bringing unwanted attention to our whereabouts."

"He has a point." Agent Sloan looked at Levi.

Agent Montgomery shook his head. "But Ash, you should be at the hospital with Alexa."

"The doctor said she needs rest," Ash replied. "And while she is obeying the doctor's orders, I want to stop the man who is ruining my name."

Agent Sloan gave Ash a sharp nod. "Your father gave me a map of where the mine is located. Fill up your canteen, we need to leave now before it gets any later. The mine is about an hour south of here." The agent took one step away before looking back at Ash. "And leave the chasing to us."

"Yes, sir." Ash exhaled a deep breath, relieved that they agreed. He would have fought them regardless, but it was good to know they were on his side now.

As they mounted their horses, Ash could tell Agent Montgomery wasn't too pleased. He did everything he could do not to look at Ash. The man must have finally come to terms that he had lost in the fight for Alexa. Hopefully the man wasn't being too hard on himself for shooting Alexa. He really was a good agent.

The sun was high in the afternoon sky. If the temperatures kept getting warmer, Granger Pass would open again. He couldn't help but wonder if Alexa would leave and return to her family to continue her recovery. Then another thought crossed his mind, what would Mrs. O'Leary do without her husband running the ranch? All that money and items stolen would need to be returned to the rightful owners. Maybe Alexa's father would get his money back and his name would be in good standing with the people who had abandoned him. With any luck, Alexa's brother would get the money needed to help him walk.

Ash knew one thing, as soon as Alexa was feeling better, they would get married. Of course, he had to be patient and wait for that day, even as difficult as it would be. But if she wanted to become a Pinkerton agent, he would have to travel with her when she tracked down criminals. There was no way Ash wanted them to be apart again.

When the men approached the mine, Ash could sense a feeling of recognition. Memories came back of riding with his pa to meet PaPaw for lunch. He couldn't believe that after all these years, the mine was still producing moonstones. How much had his PaPaw mined during Ash's absence?

"Tie the horses here." Ash pointed to a large grove of trees. "The view in this location is hidden from the main road."

They dismounted and tied their horses around the limbs of the tree. Not too far off was an entrance to the mine. Ash pointed toward it. "We enter through there."

As the three men headed to the opening, Dusty stopped, holding up his arm. Right inside the entrance was a horse. Ash's chest tightened as anger rose inside him again. The robber was already there.

Levi pulled out his gun, checking it to make sure it was loaded. Dusty bunched his knuckles a few times, as if he were planning on offering up a strong punch or two at the intruder. Dusty nodded and the three took careful steps to make sure they wouldn't be spotted.

Ash felt a little out of place since he didn't carry a gun. But that was fine with him. He had a skill the agents didn't have. Ash knew how to use a mining pick.

Immediately, he noticed the very item leaning against the mine's wall. As he passed it, he grabbed it without Levi or Dusty seeing him.

"From my slim recollection," Ash said quietly, "the tunnel goes straight, and then downward. I'm sure a lot has changed over the years, so watch your step and be careful."

"It's so dark in here," Levi commented.

"You will get used to it." Ash paused. "I have an idea. Since you can't see very well, I will go inside and lure the person out. Then you both will be here waiting for him."

Dusty had a not-so-sure look on his face, but Levi quickly nodded. "Don't be long. Get him out of there quickly."

Part of Ash wondered if Levi hoped he would get hurt and die while in the mine so the agent could have Alexa all to himself. Then again, Ash knew she loved him, and that knowledge would keep him safe.

Moonstone and Mistrust

Ash took quick steps inside the mine, following the route that seemed most familiar to him as a child. It didn't take long for his vision to grow accustomed to the darkness. A tiny bit of suffocation crept over him, and he could hear Bowser yelling at the boys to work harder and stop talking.

Shaking away the nightmarish thoughts, Ash told himself he was doing this for Alexa and her family. Justice needed to be served, and he wanted to be the one to do it. He was a free man, and no one would capture him again, and nothing—not even going into a mine—would frighten him ever again.

Suddenly, he heard a cart moving on the rails. It sounded as if it were coming his way. He quickened his steps forward to the sound. Raising the pick above his head, he prepared for the attack. The shadow of the man pushing the cart came into view. Gripping the handle, Ash waited to strike.

When he saw the man and recognition hit, Ash about lost his breath from the surprise. He couldn't believe his eyes. Why in the world would Jeremiah Jones be here?

When his old so-called *friend* saw Ash, he stopped and his mouth hung open.

"Hawk? Is that yer face I'm seein'?"

Ash gritted his teeth. "It's my face, Jones, but I think *you* are going by Hawk now, and not me."

Jeremiah laughed forcefully. "I don't know what ye mean."

"Why are you here at Hawkins Gem?" Ash lowered the pickaxe slightly but gripped the handle tighter.

"Big Ed took our lives away. I want mine back."

Ash shook his head. "But you are robbing people of their livelihood. How is that getting *your* life back? The way it looks to me, you will be spending your life behind bars soon."

"It won't. This isn't my first theft, and it won't be my last. You should join us." Jeremiah stepped around the cart. "Gunther O'Leary and I make a great team, but if ye help us, we'll be unstoppable."

Ash chuckled. Jeremiah had no clue O'Leary was caught. "No. This isn't life for me. Settling down with a wife and family is all I want now."

"Well, if ye ain't helpin', then get out the way." Jeremiah pulled on the cart, putting it into movement again.

"You never told me why you're using my name." Ash arched his brows. "What did I ever do to you to make you want to ruin me?"

"Nuthin' really." He shrugged. "Hawk just sounded like a good bank robber's name."

Ash stepped aside, letting Jeremiah push the cart past him. Now the man was trapped and didn't even know it. Yet.

Just before they reached the cave's opening, Ash snickered. "Jones, I forgot to tell you Gunther won't be joining you tonight, or any other time. He told me to tell you he would see you in jail."

Just then Dusty and Levi stepped out of their hiding spots in the darkness with their guns pointed at Jeremiah. He stopped and tried to push back. Ash swung the pickaxe, and the solid part of the tool connected to Jeremiah's jaw, sending him into a spinning whirl before falling into the cart.

Levi rushed over and cuffed Jeremiah while Dusty kept his gun pointed at the criminal. Ash grinned. Now he knew *two* purposes for a pickaxe.

Dusty patted Ash on the back as they walked out. "Good job."

"Yeah, but how did they know about this particular mine? Nobody knew that the owners were my parents. I didn't even know until yesterday."

Levi glared at Jeremiah and yanked on his cuffed hands. "Who else are you working with?"

The look on Jeremiah's face was pure panic. Blood was oozing from his chin where Ash had hit him.

"She made me do it," Jeremiah blubbered.

"Who?" Dusty asked.

"Mrs. O'Leary. I met her in Durango. She could see I was down on my luck, and she said she'd pay me fifty bucks if I robbed a little bank in town. So, I did. She paid me the money and asked if I wanted more. When I realized how easy it was, she took me back to Utah. There was a bigger bank in Santaquin. That was the motherload."

"He is telling the truth," Ash said. "When I made it to Longmont, to the O'Leary's ranch, Gunther said his wife was visiting family in Utah and would be back at the end of the month. That was when I started seeing new things pop up inside the house."

"I saw ye workin' there," Jeremiah told Ash. "I was goin' to stay and work at the ranch with ya but decided against it. That was when I decided to use yer name. Ya had so many friends, and I had none."

Dusty's expression hardened. "When we get back to town, I think we need to go pay Mrs. O'Leary a visit. Right, Agent Montgomery?"

"I hope she hasn't run yet," Ash said. "After all, her husband was arrested very early this morning."

Jeremiah shook his head. "She won't run. She is waitin' for me at the house. I had hoped that ye'd be caught instead of me. That was why I told that pretty Pinkerton agent where to find ye."

"What pretty agent?" Levi snapped.

"The woman. Agent Moore."

Ash wanted to laugh. He wouldn't tell Jeremiah the truth about her identity, especially since he figured that once she recovered, she would become an agent soon.

Levi pushed Jeremiah toward the horse. "Get on."

After they all mounted, Dusty held the reins of Jeremiah's horse, and they trotted back to Longmont.

"Now what are you going to do when we get back home?" Levi asked Ash.

"I'm going to tell Alexa the good news. She will be happy to know everyone has been caught and her father's items can be returned." Ash grinned, feeling accomplished.

"I think there is another thing you should do," Levi said.

"What's that?" Ash looked over at Levi.

Agent Montgomery smiled. "Ask Alexa to marry you. Because if you don't, I will."

Ash chuckled. "I already have, and she said yes."

Growling, Levi kicked the sides of his horse and rode ahead of Ash. He almost felt sorry for the man but instead, he was elated that he was being blessed yet again.

EIGHTEEN

"I now pronounce you husband and wife." Pastor Williams smiled widely as his attention jumped between Alexa and Ash. "You may now kiss the bride."

Ash grinned. "I thought you would never ask."

When Ash wrapped her in his arms so quickly, she laughed, but the moment his mouth covered hers, she melted against him and kissed him back, even though it couldn't be very passionate. Not while in a church with a crowd of people witnessing their marriage.

She never thought this day would come. It took nearly six weeks for her to recover enough to walk around the yard without getting weak. Ash's wonderful parents let her stay with them in their large home, and also invited her own family to come. Ma tried to make Alexa feel guilty for not going home with them, but she didn't want to be away from the man she loved ever again.

The guests started cheering, which was the cue to stop the kiss. She would definitely pick up where they left off tonight when they were alone. The afternoon reception would pass by slowly, she just knew it.

Ash kept her in his arms as they turned toward their guests. He punched a fist in the air, feeling victorious, making half of the crowd cheer louder. She wanted to do that as well but feared her injured shoulder wouldn't allow it yet.

The church had been decorated with ribbons and bows, thanks to both sets of parents. But it wasn't the decorations that made her feel like the prettiest woman in Colorado. It was the way her handsome husband gazed at her as if he had never seen anything prettier.

Alexa had worn her mother's wedding gown, with only a few alterations. Although Ash's parents offered to buy her a new gown, she wanted to keep with tradition and wear the wedding dress her mother wore which was Alexa's maternal grandmother's as well.

Ash released her, only to take her hand as they headed out of the church. Once outside, people tossed rice at them, making them laugh harder. He took her back into his arms, kissing her one more time. She would never get tired of this man's passion.

"Well, Mrs. Hawkins," Ash said softly. "Are you regretting the decision to marry me yet?"

She shook her head. "If you hadn't asked me, I would have asked you." She caressed the side of his face. "I fell hard for you, and nothing could change that—even when I thought you were a criminal."

"Thanks for believing in me."

She shrugged her good shoulder. "I'm sorry it took a minute for me to realize you weren't a criminal."

"I love you, Mrs. Hawkins." He kissed her forehead.

"And I love you, Mr. Hawkins." She cocked her head. "Although, I think I want to be called Mrs. Hawk, instead."

He laughed. "Maybe when we are alone, we can do that."

"Yes, I would like that."

Sighing, she leaned against him, watching the guests converse with each other. "When should we return to your family's house?"

"The reception will start in an hour. That will give us time to arrive and get cleaned up before the big party."

She pulled back enough to look into his intoxicating green eyes. "I wish we didn't have to. I just want to be with you, and only you."

His grin stretched wider. "That is what the wedding night is for, you know, along with the honeymoon."

She laughed. "Then I suppose I will have to endure being with other people until the sun goes down."

Moonstone and Mistrust

"If I can do it, so can you, and believe me, this night has been on my mind since I proposed marriage."

She waggled her eyebrows. "That makes two of us." She paused. "I don't think you told me, but were you planning on running the Moonstone mine for your parents?"

"My father told me it is mine when I'm ready, but…" Ash sighed heavily. "After working in a mine for most of my life, I'm not ready to go back. There are too many bad memories."

Her heart softened with empathy. "I don't blame you one bit."

"But I'm still considering it. After all, I need to provide for my wife, and the children we will soon have."

"We don't need to think about that right now. Let us just enjoy our special day."

His gaze dropped to her mouth. "Oh, believe me, I will enjoy every moment with you for the rest of our lives."

From behind her, she heard a man clearing his throat. At first, she wanted to get upset for whoever was interrupting her private time with her husband, but then she realized the guests were here to celebrate along with the newlyweds.

Before she could turn, Ash straightened and gave the man a nod.

"Agent Sloan," Ash said. "It's good of you to come to our wedding."

Dusty's smile was genuine as he shook Ash's hand, and then hers. "I wouldn't have missed this for the world."

She glanced around him, wondering if Levi had come with him. She knew Levi hadn't meant to shoot her, and although it was still upsetting that he wanted to kill Ash, she was working on trying to forgive him. She hadn't seen him since that awful night when he shot her, but Ash said the Pinkerton agent was at the hospital and feeling terrible about what had happened.

"It is good to see you, Agent Sloan," she said sweetly. "Did Agent Montgomery come with you?"

"No. Agent Montgomery decided to move to New York where his family is from."

Part of her wanted to be sad that he never said goodbye, but then she hadn't completely forgiven him, so maybe she would travel to New York when she was ready to talk to him again. "That is too bad he couldn't come."

"Yes, he was a good agent, but now that he is gone, that leaves an opening in the office." Dusty folded his arms across his chest. "I was very impressed by the work you did in trying to find the bank robbers, and I believe you would make a great agent. So, as part of your wedding gift, I'm offering you the position."

Alexa hitched a breath, but she couldn't take her eyes off Dusty. Finally, she was able to prove her worth to the Pinkertons. But… Why wasn't she more excited? This was something she wanted to do even before she married her first husband. She enjoyed the thrill of tracking down the criminals, and especially, catching them. Then she realized there was something she wanted even more than that. Being Ash's wife and the mother of his children would make her complete. Once the children started coming, she didn't want to do anything to put them in danger, and being a Pinkerton agent was not an easy job.

She couldn't believe she was going to say it. In fact, hearing the words in her head almost made her laugh.

"Agent Sloan, I'm very happy for your exceptional offer, however…" She looked at her husband whose eyes were wide with curiosity. "I don't think I will take the position. I'm very happy being Ash's wife."

Surprise registered on her husband's face, and she almost laughed then. Apparently, he didn't want her to be a Pinkerton agent, either.

"Well," Dusty said, "I suppose I will have to find someone else. But if you ever change your mind, let me know."

She turned her attention back to the agent. "Thank you again. You don't know how much I appreciate your offer, nonetheless."

Dusty's gaze moved to Ash. "As for you, Mr. Hawkins, I have a situation I need help with."

Ash's eyes widened even more. "You need *my* help with something?"

"Indeed, I do. I don't know who else to talk with about this problem. You see, once we arrested Mr. and Mrs. O'Leary, they had to give up all of their assets, and their ranch—and everything on the land—goes with it. Because they have no family, the state of Colorado doesn't know what to do with it. I suggested that you, Mr. Hawkins, might like to own the ranch since you enjoyed working there so much."

Alexa gasped and turned toward her husband, grasping his waist-jacket. He stared at the agent with a dropped jaw. Happiness grew inside her, bursting at the seams. Dusty Sloan was certainly giving them an unexpected wedding gift.

"Well?" Dusty asked. "What do you think?"

A gush of air released from Ash's throat as if he had been holding his breath. "You are going to *give* me the ranch and everything that goes with it?"

Dusty nodded. "Everything. Even the ranch hands if they want to work for you."

Laughing, Ash gathered her closer as he stared into her eyes. Her heart melted. She loved seeing him so excited.

"What do you think?" Ash asked.

"You know what I think." She grinned. "And I know what a wonderful landowner you will be."

"Will you help me?"

She nodded. "Any way I can, of course."

Turning back toward Dusty, Ash squared his shoulders and stuck out his right hand. "Agent Sloan, I would love to be the ranch's owner. But can I change the name?"

"Certainly."

Ash cupped the side of her face. "I would like to call the ranch, *Hawk's Heaven*."

Her heart melted even more. "That is the perfect name for our ranch."

"You inspire me, my love."

How many times was this wonderful man going to cause her knees to weaken? She hoped he continued making her feel this giddy for the rest of their lives.

"I love you, Ashton Hawkins, and I always will."

His gaze softened, making his eyes turn greener. Heavens, his eyes were the perfect color. She hoped their children had eyes like his.

He lowered his mouth to hers, forgetting about the man who watched, and kissed her passionately. She threw her arms around Ash's neck and answered back, not caring who saw her. After all, this was their special day, and as each minute passed, the excitement—and anticipation—inside of her only grew bigger.

Of course, what did she expect? She had married the best man in the world.

THE END

READERS…

We thank you so much for devotedly following the Gems of the West series. Although we are sad to see the series end, we are delighted to introduce you to the spin-off series, *Love's Wager*, where incidentally, Agent Levi Montgomery will be our hero.

In this new series, we have decided to start a penname (which we should have done for the *Gems of the West* series, but we didn't think of it soon enough). For our historical stories, we are using the name Scarlett Monroe, a name we came up with when we were young and playing Barbies.

Here is the prologue and first chapter of "Gretta's Gamble". See all the book covers for this awesome series here – https://www.authormariehiggins.com/love-s-wager-american-historical

Love's Wager Series info:

To keep their carefree bachelor lives, these childhood friends create a wager—that they will never marry. The first man to marry will forfeit something of great value. Will they remain strong when they find that one woman who drives them insane and yet cannot keep away from?

Other published stories by Marie Higgins

https://www.authormariehiggins.com/books

Other published stories by Stacey Haynes

https://www.amazon.com/Stacey-Haynes/e/B088NTQQPJ

Join Marie's newsletter and add to your reading collection -

https://www.authormariehiggins.com/newsletter

MARIE'S BIO

Marie Higgins is a best-selling, multi-published author of Christian and sweet romance novels; from refined bad-boy heroes who make your heart melt to the feisty heroines who somehow manage to love them regardless of their faults. She's been with a Christian publisher since 2010. Between those and her others, she's published over 100 heartwarming, on-the-edge-of-your-seat stories and broadened her readership by writing mystery/suspense, humor, time-travel, paranormal, along with her love for historical romances. Her readers have dubbed her "Queen of Tease", because of all her twists and turns and unexpected endings.

Visit her website to discover more about her – https://authormariehiggins.com

STACEY'S BIO

Stacey Haynes is an award-winning, and best-selling author. She has always enjoyed reading and writing romance stories beginning with her first story in 6th grade. Her dream has always been to have one of her books published, and now she has several, including a poem about her most disliked food, Peas!

She won her first writing contest when she and her sister, Marie, entered their story The Magic of a Billionaire into an online writing contest on www.ajoara.com – and their story won 1st place!

She considers herself a hopeless romantic and tries to find the best in others. She loves to write in her spare time to relax after a hard day at work.

Stacey lives in Utah with her wonderful husband and three adorable children. She hopes to have more books published in her lifetime.

You can follow her adventures on Facebook – http://www.facebook.com/StaceyHaynes
https://www.facebook.com/Stacey-Haynes-Author-110345070332647
Instagram – https://www.instagram.com/Staceybuns1969/
Bookbub – https://www.bookbub.com/authors/stacey-haynes

Made in the USA
Coppell, TX
19 September 2023